Meredith Webber lives on the sunny Gold Coast in Queensland, Australia, but takes regular trips west into the Outback, fossicking for gold or opal. These breaks in the beautiful and sometimes cruel red earth country provide her with an escape from the writing desk and a chance for her mind to roam free— not to mention getting some much needed exercise. They also supply the kernels of so many stories that it's hard for her to stop writing!

HEALED BY
HER ARMY DOC

MEREDITH WEBBER

MILLS & BOON

First published in Great Britain 2018
by Mills & Boon, an imprint of HarperCollins*Publishers*
1 London Bridge Street, London, SE1 9GF

Large Print edition 2019

© 2018 Meredith Webber

ISBN: 978-0-263-07806-0

MIX
Paper from
responsible sources
FSC **FSC C007454**

This book is produced from independently certified
FSC™ paper to ensure responsible forest management. For
more information visit www.harpercollins.co.uk/green.

Printed and bound in Great Britain
by CPI Group (UK) Ltd, Croydon, CR0 4YY

CHAPTER ONE

SHE MIGHT BE Kate's favourite relative and most stalwart support, but Aunt Alice was adept at catching Kate in unguarded moments and tonight was no exception.

'You've only worked a half-shift today, and you're off duty tomorrow, so it couldn't be better, *and* you've got the excuse of that team meeting you had this afternoon,' Alice pointed out.

The team meeting that afternoon was the reason Kate was unguarded, though flummoxed would have been a better word. Arriving late from Theatre, still pulling off her theatre cap and running her fingers through her chaotic, needing-a-cut hair, she'd rushed into the SDR meeting room, and the first person Kate had seen had been Angus.

Not surprising, the seeing part. Men who stood just over six feet tall and had the shoulders that went with the height weren't easy to miss.

But Angus?

Here!

Shock halted her momentarily, then, as her bones had turned to jelly, she'd subsided into the nearest seat, rather wishing her weight would take it straight down through the floor.

Or there'd be an earthquake, tornado, hospital on fire—any distraction…

The worst of it was that whatever had flared between them three years ago on the island was just as electrifyingly alive as it had been back then. She could feel that inexplicable awareness that had rocked both of them arcing across the room between them. Looked up to check she couldn't actually see it in the form of flashing lightning because she'd heard it in the thunder in her veins.

Angus!

'You can tell Harriet what was discussed,' Alice was persisting, bringing Kate out of the horrendous memories of the afternoon meeting of the Specialist Disaster Response team. 'She's really down about missing it, well, not the meeting so much but as being part of the team. She could have gone to the meeting, but I think that Pete was supposed to collect her and, as far as I can make out, he's been conspicuous by his absence lately.'

Not much got past Alice, who, although unconnected to the hospital, was a long-term resident of the apartment block where so many of the staff lived.

In her head Kate acknowledged her great-aunt was right, and not only about Harriet's boyfriend disappearing. Before she'd injured her leg in an accident on a training day for the SDR, Harriet had been an integral and enthusiastic part of the team but after battling operations and infections she must be wondering if she'd ever be able to join it again, while she and Pete had been one of the glamour couples of Bondi Bayside Hospital's social scene.

Not that Kate was part of that scene, but in any hospital there were few secrets.

'Go on,' Alice was saying. 'You've lived here two years, you work at the same hospital, belong to that team together, and you barely know Harriet. You can't shut yourself away for ever—it's just not natural. She probably thinks you're a terrible snob because you're a surgeon and she's only a nurse.'

'Hardly "only" a nurse, Alice,' Kate said. 'She's one of the top nurses in the ICU and that's probably one of the most important jobs in the whole hospital.'

Kate was glad of the conversation—anything to keep her mind off the SDR meeting.

Off Angus!

He *can't* be here!

He is!

She dragged her mind back to the subject of Alice's conversation, to Harriet Collins.

'Intensive Care is high-level nursing. It's just that with work and study and keeping up the level of fitness I need to stay on the team I don't really have time—'

'Tosh!' said Alice. 'You're hiding away from something—from life itself, in fact. I know you needed to grieve for the baby, that's why I asked you to come and live here with me. New hospital, new job, new people—but you should have moved on by now. This self-imposed isolation of yours has gone on long enough. So get over to Harriet's apartment and tell her about the meeting. Find a way to convince her she'll get back on the team before long.'

Knowing it was futile to argue, Kate had a quick shower, washed her hair, pulled on jeans and a light sweatshirt and made her way along the corridor to Harriet's apartment, her feet beating out an accompaniment to the phrase running over and over in her head.

I will not think about Angus, it went. I will *not* think about Angus. I *will* not think about Angus...

Harriet's apartment was at the front of the block so as Harriet opened the door—more than slightly startled—Kate could see straight through the living room to the ocean beyond, painted pale pink and violet as it reflected the colours of the sky at sunset.

'Kate!'

The exclamation told Kate she'd guessed right, although she now substituted 'extremely' for the 'slightly' in the startled stakes.

'I hope I'm not interrupting you but I thought you might like to know what went on at the meeting.'

Harriet stared at her and seeing the blankness in her hazel eyes, and the pale drawn skin beneath the lovely auburn hair, Kate had to set aside her own preoccupation and accept that Alice—as ever—had been right. All was not well with the usually vibrant Harriet.

'So, can I come in?'

Wordlessly, Harriet stepped back and waved her hand towards the living room.

'What a fantastic view! You take in the whole bay. It's unbelievable. You must see the beach and ocean in so many moods. Are you a photographer? You could take a thousand pictures from your balcony with not one of them the same.'

Kate knew she was blethering, but Harriet's silence was unnerving and she'd already been totally unnerved once today.

'Did Alice send you to cheer me up?'

Not exactly the conversation opener Kate had expected but it would do.

'Yes, she did. She's worried about you. We're all worried about you.'

Deep breath!

'Actually, to be honest, she's worried about me too. She thinks I work too hard, but the SDR meeting *was* interesting. Blake had brought along an army bloke who has been working on a new emergency response tent. You know, one of those ones that fold up and can be dropped into disaster zones and comes complete with all our medical needs. Apparently, he has a new prototype he wants to trial next time we have a callout to somewhere fairly isolated.'

'Not close to a local hospital or, say, in a bushfire where the hospital's been damaged or destroyed,' Harriet said, picking up on the idea immediately. 'I've seen army ones on exercises we've taken with other teams. They really are a complete package, right down to food, water and accommodation for the first responders— enough for them to be self-sufficient for a fortnight.'

Taking the words as a small spark of interest, Kate said, 'Shall I tell you about it? Will we sit down?'

Harriet was frowning slightly, but as Kate perched on the sofa, her hostess dropped into an armchair. The frown was understandable. Here was this neighbour, who'd been in the apartment block for two years yet had never ventured over the threshold, making herself at home.

And talking, talking, talking—

The doorbell shrilled, and Harriet's frown deepened.

'It must be someone from another apartment because they didn't ring at the front door.'

It shrilled again.

'Would you like me to get it?' Kate offered, her heart going out to the woman she'd only known as lively and active, now a pale shadow of her former self.

A shadow with her injured leg still in its ungainly brace.

'No, I'll go.'

Harriet rose to her feet and limped to the door, opening it to reveal the person Kate was still telling herself not to think about.

'I'm sorry to disturb you,' came the deep growl from the doorway. 'I'm Angus Caruth, and Blake gave me Kate's address, and then Alice said she was here and that you wouldn't mind if I popped in to say hello. I barely recognised her earlier, at the meeting. I don't think I'd ever seen Kate with dry hair.'

Kate's gut had twisted more with every word he spoke, but she'd regained some control over her mind, so as Harriet ushered in her new visitor, she used anger to mask all the other reactions that had rioted inside her since the meeting.

'Blake gave you my address?' she demanded. 'Whatever happened to staff confidentiality?'

'Oh, I'd blame Sam for that,' Harriet said, obviously intrigued by this second visitor. She waved her arm towards the sofa, and invited Angus to sit. 'Ever since she and Blake got together, she's been seeing the world through a pearly haze of love.'

She turned to Kate and smiled—smiled properly!

'So what's with the wet hair?'

The smile was the first sign of the old Harriet that Kate had seen so she felt obliged to reply.

'Angus and I met in a cyclone. Everyone had wet hair.'

She kept her eyes on Harriet as she spoke, for all the good that did her. Her body was as aware of Angus as it would have been if he had been sitting on top of her—her skin prickling with something she'd rather call discomfort than—

No, it couldn't possibly be attraction...

How could this have happened?

Why did it have to be her hospital he'd turned up at?

And why, after all this time, could he still affect her like this?

But now he was talking again, and if she closed her eyes—

She straightened in her seat.

'"Angus and I met in a cyclone" hardly covers it,' he was responding, smiling at her before turning to Harriet. 'We were stuck in the dining room of a resort hotel and a tree had crashed into one glass wall, so we had about sixty panicking people to deal with. Kate calmly organised the wait staff to tear tablecloths into bandages and once we had all the injured settled as well as we could, she started everyone singing. I think trying to manage "Come to dinner" sung in four parts certainly took their minds off the howling gale and thunderous winds outside.'

Refusing to yield to the memories, Kate tried desperately to ignore the man on the sofa beside her—to ignore all the signals that were zapping between their bodies.

She had to get away, to sort out what was happening and why, after three years, she should still feel this way about a man she barely knew.

It was the coward's way out but she turned to Harriet.

'Angus is the man I was telling you about, the one with the new tent, and now he's here, he can tell you about it himself.'

She pushed herself to her feet, hoping her face wasn't revealing the torrent of emotions roaring inside her—hoping her legs would hold her up and, most of all, hoping Angus couldn't see the quivering mess his presence had made of her body.

'I really should go,' she added. 'It's my turn to cook dinner.'

She strode to the door, opening it and pausing briefly to waggle her fingers in farewell.

And to take in the face of the man who'd haunted her dreams for the past three years.

Angus!

Closing the door behind her, she leant against the wall in the hall, eyes shut so she could see him again on her eyelids—check him against her memories.

No, he hadn't changed. Still the same dark, almost shorn hair, black quirky eyebrows above deep-set blue eyes, slightly crooked nose, the result she knew of a youthful brawl, and lips—

She wouldn't think about his lips—not the shape of them, or the paleness, or the way they'd felt as they'd brushed across her skin...

Her heart fluttered and for a moment she was back on the island—back in his arms—lost in blissful sensation...

She pushed angrily away from the wall. How dared Blake Cooper give out her address? How dared Angus walk back into her life like this?

Angus felt her absence, which was ridiculous given he hadn't seen her for three years, for all he'd thought about her. Wondering where she was, what she was doing, thinking about contacting her, but how?

And why?

To hurt her as he'd hurt Michelle—never being there for her when she'd needed him, never considering just how hard their separations had been for her?

This new project would take him away even more. Their orders to leave would come within twenty-four hours of a disaster occurring somewhere in the world. Here today and gone tomorrow—how fair was that on any woman, let alone one he'd come to remember as special...?

Then she'd rushed into the SDR room where he had been explaining the new emergency structure, her fingers flipping her hair into a dark halo around her head.

Too far away to see the pale blue-grey of her eyes, but aware they'd widened in shock—

'I'd rather hear about the cyclone than the tent.'

Harriet's words made him realise he was still staring at the door through which Kate had vanished.

He caught the speculative gleam in Harriet's eyes and smiled at her.

'About the cyclone or about Kate Mitchell?' he asked, and Harriet blushed.

'Well, she *has* always been something of a mystery woman,' she admitted. 'I imagine the army is a bit like a hospital where everyone knows everyone else's business, but Kate...'

She shrugged.

'Perhaps we're better talking about the tent.'

Angus smiled again and agreed, although his mind was whirling with questions. Kate a bit of a mystery woman? Blake Cooper had given much the same impression. A loner, he'd said. Yet the Kate Angus remembered had been outgoing and cheerful, shrugging off the pain she must have been feeling when she'd joked about honeymooning alone on the island.

'Well, I'd booked it and paid for it, why shouldn't I enjoy it?' she'd said with a smile that had belied the cloudy sadness in her eyes.

Had he hurt her more?

Caused the change?

Surely not, but something had...

He turned his attention back to Harriet.

'You probably know all about regular emergency structures but most of them are intended for long-term use, say after an earthquake. The "tent", as Kate called it, is a smaller affair— an inflatable, easily set-up protected area that combines a trauma unit to act as the ED, a surgical theatre for life-and-limb-saving surgery, and a multifunction unit with drugs and blood products, facilities for lab tests, and sterilisation support. Some of these are "add-on" units in other emergency set-ups, but what we've tried to do is provide the best facility possible for first response units like your SDR.'

'That makes sense,' Harriet said. 'Most patients are airlifted, or taken by road transport once they're stabilised, so you wouldn't need an intensive care unit or ward beds like some I've seen. It sounds like a great idea.'

'It's only a great idea if it works,' Angus told her. 'I've been planning and organising the construction of this one for some time, but I've only recently been posted to a base on the outskirts of Sydney. I knew Blake back when I was studying medicine so when I heard about his—well, the hospital's—SDR team I hooked up with him, hoping maybe we could get to trial it.'

He paused, then added, 'Not that I'm looking for a disaster—heaven forbid—but things happen, don't they?'

Harriet gave him a weak smile and pointed to her leg.

'Don't they just,' she said, and a finality in the words finished the conversation.

Could he go? Just stand up and walk out? Say goodbye, of course—but even if he went, could he go back to Kate's—or Alice's—apartment? He doubted he'd be welcomed. Kate had been out the door here before he'd got settled on the sofa.

He stood up.

'I'd better go,' he said. 'I do hope you get

back on the team before long. You might even get to try out my "tent".'

But Harriet didn't respond and he'd seen enough PTSD cases to know that even if she hadn't been diagnosed with it, she was deeply depressed. She'd made all the right noises when he'd first come in and even shown interest in his knowing Kate, but that short stint of casual conversation had taken all her energy.

And although he wanted nothing more than to go back to Alice's apartment and see Kate, he sat down again.

'How long since you hurt your leg?' he asked, watching her face so he could read the argument going on in her head about whether or not she would answer.

Politeness won.

'Months now—I've lost count. I got a post-op infection that knocked me back, and the rehab seems to go on for ever.'

'You'll get there,' he said. 'You've got to keep believing that you will. Don't give up. Giving up's easy, it's sticking it out that's hard, but in the end, it's worth it. The inner strength you gain will make you a better nurse and better SDR team member.'

'And a better person? Did you forget that bit?' Harriet asked, but at least she was smiling again.

'Don't know about that, but seeing medicine from the other side definitely improves your understanding of patients and what they are going through.'

'Been there yourself?'

He smiled and shook his head.

'Close enough,' he told her, remembering the long bleak months after his last posting, part of a humanitarian response team to an overcrowded refugee camp in South-East Asia. Some of the things he'd seen—the stories he'd heard—had made him wonder if he'd ever feel normal again.

'And Kate?'

'Nice try,' he said, as Harriet's teasing smile told him he could leave with an easier conscience. He'd jolted her out of her dark mood, although for how long he didn't know.

He said goodbye, adding that he hoped they'd meet again, and was pleased when she roused herself enough to walk to the door with him.

As he left he realised he had an excuse to talk to Kate again—he could knock on the apartment door, mention his concern about Harriet's mental state.

It was a weak excuse and she'd see it that way, but having met up with her again he knew he—

What?

Wanted to see more of her?

Yes, there was that—definitely—but...

What he really wanted to know was what had changed her from the woman who'd smiled through the pain of the end of her relationship, who'd settled terrified guests with a warm word and a joke during the cyclone, who'd been friendly and outgoing and...

Well, fun!

Back when he'd met her, she'd have had every reason to be withdrawn. She'd discovered her best friend had been sleeping with her fiancé and had broken off the engagement, heading for the island to escape the talk.

But she'd taken one look at his pale face on the island boat and made him stay on deck, explaining it was far better to be outside than in if you felt the slightest bit queasy. So they'd clung to the rail, salt spray washing over them both, and she'd kept his mind off the journey, telling him about the little coral cay that lay ahead, and the research station on it that she'd visited each year with her great-aunt Alice, a marine biologist.

Alice!

The great-aunt!

By the time they'd reached the island he'd re-alised Alice probably meant more to Kate than her parents, and now here she was, living with Alice—a 'loner'!

Because?

He realised that, in spite of all they'd been through together, he didn't really know her.

He looked around the elevator lobby, and finally pressed the 'down' button.

Kate did her best to concentrate on cooking the chicken breasts in lemon and capers that was one of Alice's favourite dinners, but she'd made it so often it couldn't distract her enough.

Why wasn't Angus wearing a wedding ring?

Hadn't he gone to the island to check it out as a place for his and Michelle's honeymoon?

They'd joked on that terribly rough boat trip that they were both on pretend honeymoons, talking to take their minds off the wild seas.

And the cyclone hadn't even been close at

that stage. It was only two days later it changed direction—as cyclones so often do—and headed straight for the island.

Maybe army personnel didn't wear wedding rings, she decided. Some kind of safety thing? Could a light flashing off a gold or silver ring tell a sniper where to shoot?

Kate shook her head as she turned the capers in the frying pan, crisping them nicely. Think about the capers, not have ridiculous thoughts about snipers. Angus had been based in Townsville, anyway, and she doubted he'd have been bothered by snipers there.

Angus.

'You burning those capers, Kate?'

Surely not! She looked down at the pan, forcing her mind away from the man who'd come back so unexpectedly—shockingly, really—into her life.

'No, but you like them crisp. Nearly ready!'

She put the thin slices of chicken breast back into the pan, with the lemon juice and zest, swirled it around, then served them onto the waiting plates. The bowl of salad was already on the table, and Alice joined her there as she set down the plates.

They ate in silence for a few minutes, savouring the tasty food, but Kate could hear the wheels turning in Alice's head as she decided how to phrase the question Kate knew she would ask.

Except she didn't ask a question, instead issuing a statement.

'So that was the man who caused you all the trouble!'

Kate shrugged.

'He wasn't to blame for anything,' she said quietly.

'Oh, so you got pregnant all by yourself?'

Kate pushed her plate away and looked at her aunt. Great-aunt really, but they'd never made the distinction. She'd been closer to Alice than she had to her mother, had learnt more about life and the way the world worked on those holidays on the island than she'd ever learnt at home or at school.

'The getting-pregnant part was definitely my fault,' Kate admitted. 'I'd been on the Pill so didn't give a thought to the fact that I hadn't been in my room for three days during the height of the storm, which meant I hadn't been taking it. Stupid, I know, but it had been a tense time with so little sleep, and the relief of finally getting the injured and the majority of the upset tourists off the island had overwhelmed us both.'

She paused, then looked up to meet Alice's eyes.

'It was survivor sex, if that makes sense, yet...'

'It was more than that?' Alice asked gently.

Kate nodded.

'It seemed that way,' she murmured, a little of the remembered passion sparking to life inside her. 'We'd been through so much together, it was as if we had a...bond, I suppose, is the only way to describe it. A special bond.'

'Didn't you tell him you were pregnant, get in touch with him?'

Kate shuddered as she remembered the anguish of those early days.

'How could I? I'd done exactly what my best friend had done—slept with someone else's fiancé—and that had broken up my marriage plans. Should I break up his as well?'

She sighed.

'In the end, I knew it wasn't right to *not* tell him so I kind of left it up to him. I sent him a note, care of the base in Townsville, just asking if he'd like to give me a call—gave him my number. I never heard anything after that, which, I think, given all that happened, was for the best, don't you?'

Alice shook her head.

Angus made his way back towards the hospital where he'd left his car, his left hand in his pocket, fingering the card Blake had given him.

Some impulse made him stop and look around at the dark water of the ocean disappearing into the night, at the sand, patterned in shadows by the street lights on the esplanade. He breathed deeply, drawing in the salty tang of the air that only existed this close to the beach.

He was a free agent at the moment, at the beginning of an untimed trip to talk to groups like Bondi Bayside's SDR all over Australia. He'd started here because it was closest to his army base, intending to find a hotel in Sydney to use while he covered the other response teams and government officials he needed to see. But wasn't that a hotel? Just across the road from the apartments? Bondi wasn't so far out of Sydney city that he couldn't base himself here for the local appointments.

He pulled out Blake's card and phoned him, inordinately pleased when Blake said he was only too happy to take him on their next call-out. Another reason to stay in Bondi!

'So you can see how our system works,' Blake had added, causing a small twinge of guilt in Angus's gut. 'I'll give Mabel your mobile number. We meet at the chopper on the roof of the hospital. Check in at Reception if you get a call. I'll leave instructions for them to give you a special visitor's card that will give you access to the elevator, and allow you to go up to the roof.'

It was only when this was organised that Angus realised Kate might not be on the next SDR callout, but she *was* here, in Bondi, he'd seen her, and he had no intention of leaving until he'd seen her again. Seen her properly! If he didn't catch up with her this way, he'd have to think of something else.

Why?

The question struck him as he was about to turn away from the beach, and he couldn't brush it away.

Was it simply determination to find out why, according to the little he'd heard, she'd changed from a lively, friendly, outgoing young woman to a loner? Back then, he'd seen the shadows of sadness in her eyes, but she'd talked and laughed and even joked about her solitary honeymoon—been vibrantly alive...

Or was it because she'd somehow got beneath his skin three years ago?

Because something special, quite apart from the sex, which had been momentous, had happened between them on the island? Something had drawn them together during those terrifying hours in a way he'd never felt before?

Or since, come to that.

Until she'd walked into the SDR meeting earlier today.

Until he'd felt a surge of excitement—electrifying excitement—rush through his body...

Okay, so maybe there was more reason for him to see her again, than to find out what had changed her...

He walked back to the hospital, retrieved his vehicle from the car park and headed to the hotel, telling himself he was being foolish yet unable to persuade himself to move on. He had to see the leaders of the State Emergency Service and the Fire and Rescue Service. He'd chosen Bondi Bayside Hospital as his starting point because he'd known Blake was there, but he'd begin phoning other services in the morning, make appointments, arrange meetings. There was plenty to keep him in Sydney.

Kate was almost pleased when the phone rang in the early hours of the morning. She'd been tossing and turning all night, her sleep disturbed by memories of the island, of the fury of the cyclone, of fear...

Of Angus.

'Yes, Mabel,' she answered, knowing from the ring tone it was their SDR co-ordinator. As usual, Mabel wasted no time on pleasantries.

'RTA at a crossroads in a farming community north-west of Sydney. Road train, fortunately on its way to collect cattle, hit a car, number of passengers unknown. Blake will keep you posted as he hears more.'

Kate was pulling on her SDR overalls as she thought about the accident—road trains consisted of the huge prime mover with three double-decker trailers hooked on behind. Stopping one suddenly would be almost impossible. Although easier without the cattle…

She laced up her boots so she didn't trip as she hurried back to the hospital. Their other gear was kept in a shed on the hospital roof— helmets with headlamps and communication equipment, safety vests and the big backpacks that carried both basic first-aid and life-saving, equipment.

In a little over ten minutes she was on the hospital roof, joining the others as they snapped on protective vests, fitted their helmets and clambered on board.

Where a large man, similarly dressed, was sitting in what she thought of as 'her' seat.

Angus!

'What are you doing here?' she demanded, tasking the empty seat next to him and strapping herself in. 'We won't need your tent.'

He grinned at her, which caused a flood of unwanted reactions.

'Just wanted to see how the other half do it,' he said, and she shoved away her personal issues and shuddered as she thought of the emergencies that army medical response teams must answer. She'd seen her share of torn and damaged bodies cut from vehicle wrecks, but bodies mangled by unexpected bombs?

'Do you still do it?' she asked, as the rest of the crew settled themselves, desperate to keep things on a professional level.

He shook his head.

'Not for a while—not after the last trip.'

And something in the way he spoke told her it had been horrific. Her hand moved towards his knee then quickly retreated, although her heart ached that this was how it had to be between them.

He was obviously having no trouble with professional distance, continuing to explain his situation.

'I'm strictly home based for the moment. My last overseas posting was when I got back from the island—within a day, in fact.'

So maybe he'd never received the note she'd sent.

And why that brought a sudden blip of pleasure she didn't know.

Relief she'd have understood, but pleasure?

Because it meant he hadn't ignored it completely, you idiot, she told herself, then conversation ceased as Blake checked who was on board and the aircraft took off.

They lifted into the air, the engines settled into their customary throb, and Blake began to fill them in on what lay ahead.

'Country crossroad, no lights or signals but a stop sign for traffic in the minor road, and clear views both ways along the major road.'

'It's still dark enough for the road train to have had its lights on. It would have been hard to miss it,' Paul, one of the paramedics, remarked.

'Not our problem,' Blake reminded the speaker. 'The hows and whys are up to the police and the coroner, our job is to treat the injured. Unknown number of people in the car, which was still being extricated from the prime mover when Mabel called, then the driver of the big rig.'

'Do we know if he was carrying a passenger—his wife, or a relief driver perhaps?' someone asked, and Blake shook his head.

'The local police, fire and ambulance services will all be at the scene by the time we get there. There's a very small town with a district hospital nearby but it hasn't the facilities to handle anything serious so we'll probably be flying anyone badly injured back with us. Paul, I want you on triage. We've got an extra doc with us in Angus, the fellow some of you met the other day.'

Several heads turned to nod at Angus, while Blake, briefing over, walked forward to stand behind the pilot and air crewman so he'd see the scene from above.

'He doesn't waste words, does he?' Angus said, twisting his mike away from his face so he could talk to Kate.

'We all know the routine. Right now, he'll want to check out the terrain and see where the best place for us to set up might be. The helicopter usually puts down some distance away so people on the ground aren't affected by downdraught. We cart all our stuff to the scene in the backpacks. The ambulance on site will have its monitoring equipment already set up but in a small country town there's likely to only be one ambulance so they need us as well.'

Was she relaxing as she talked to him?

Angus hoped so.

If he wanted to find out what had gone on in

her life to change her so much, then he needed to get close to her.

And was figuring out her life over the past three years the only reason he wanted to be close to her?

Honesty forced him to admit it wasn't.

Since the seemingly endless hours they'd spent together, keeping the resort guests safe and relaxed—not to mention the night in the only dry bed on the island after the cyclone had passed—Kate had regularly sneaked into his thoughts.

Try as he might to forget her, an image of her would suddenly appear in his head, and at times she'd filled his daydreams and haunted his nights.

Even on that last traumatic posting in South-East Asia, where he'd been treating refugees, men, women and children, fleeing their country, their homes blazing behind them, and their attackers shooting at them as they fled to the nearest border to escape. Even there he'd thought of Kate far more than he'd thought of Michelle.

And his fiancée had undoubtedly picked up

on this to have broken off their engagement within days of his return.

Although telling her about Kate—about that one night of intimacy—had probably had something to do with it as well...

And now, even through the layers of clothing they both wore, he could feel the warmth of Kate's body at his side—feel a rightness in it—as if they belonged.

Kate...

CHAPTER TWO

THE CLUSTER OF strobing lights from the emergency vehicles told them they were close, although inside the cabin of the chopper all they could see were the blue and red flashes.

They put down outside the circle of light and, each grabbing a backpack, jogged closer to the scene.

'We're still cutting the vehicle free,' a policeman told them. 'The road train driver's been removed. He's in that ambulance over there.' He pointed, before adding, 'You might take a look at him. He's in a bad way.'

Blake nodded to Kate, who headed for the ambulance, disconcerted but somehow not surprised when Angus followed her.

An ambo was using a bag mask ventilator on the driver, while his fellow attendant stuck ECG leads to the man.

'GCS?' Kate asked, referring to the Glasgow

Coma Scale that measured how responsive their patient was.

'Fourteen when we got here, but he's in and out of consciousness.'

'Coupcontrecoup injury,' Kate murmured to herself as her mind pictured the scenario. The powerful rig powering through the night, then the car right there. The driver would have slammed on his brakes, and his body, held in place by a seat belt, would have stopped abruptly. But his head?

She knelt and spoke to the patient, glad to hear a response. She introduced herself and Angus, learning the patient's name was Mike.

All good so far.

'Can you remember what happened, Mike?' she asked.

'The car came flying towards the crossing, I tried to stop.'

Kate nodded, but wondered just how quickly he had stopped and whether the deceleration had caused his brain to jolt forward into the front of the skull then virtually bounce back to hit the rear.

The action could result in a serious brain injury but scanning it here would be a waste of time when it would have to be done more precisely at the hospital—and as soon as possible.

'Are you in any pain?'

'Gut hurts, and headache. The guys gave me something.'

Which probably explained why he was woozy.

'His blood pressure is dropping,' the paramedic said, nodding towards the monitor.

Kate checked the fluid line already feeding into a vein in the man's hand, then took in the abrasions to his neck and chest.

'Seat-belt syndrome,' she said to Angus, pointing out how deep the indentations were. 'With a shoulder-lap seat belt the shoulder strap took the brunt of the force. That could cause damage to the carotid. Could you check his distal pulse?'

She studied the monitor for a moment. Blood oximetry was fine, and when Angus felt a pulse in Mike's wrist, she was reassured that any loss of blood was not life-threatening.

Yet.

She examined his chest, and felt the ribs under the seat belt, but there was no palpable damage.

'Would the big rig slow for the crossing, do you know?' she asked the ambos.

They both shook their heads, but one said, 'I wouldn't think so. The place is usually deserted at night.'

'So a high-speed collision, rapid deceleration, possible internal injuries including damage to carotid artery.' She checked the fluid line again then poked her head outside the ambulance.

Paul was standing nearby.

'Possible internal bleeding from damage to the carotid. Can we lift him immediately?' she asked.

Blake, who was over to one side, watching as the car was extricated, came across, took in the information the monitor was now offering and hesitated.

'It's unlikely anyone in the car survived, but if they did, he or she will be seriously injured and will need immediate transport. We can work on them on the flight. Can you hold him a little longer?'

Kate nodded.

'We'll need to keep up the fluids and open up a bigger port in case he needs a rapid infusion,' she said to Angus as Blake hurried away.

'IO?' Angus suggested, but Kate already had the intraosseus pack in her hand and was holding the drill that would insert a needle into the bone marrow, while the ambo, who'd kept up with the exchange, was cutting their patient's shirt and opening it up.

'Here, let me,' Angus said, taking the drill from her as she used a sterile wipe to clean the site on the man's unaffected shoulder, at the head of the humerus. 'We use this more often than not in field situations,' Angus assured her, 'and I promise I've never once drilled right through the bone.'

Kate had to smile. It was always a worry, although the devices they used now for IO infusion were very sophisticated. With this access, they could deliver anticoagulant drugs to ward off a possible stroke and add high-volume drugs should the patient go into cardiac arrest.

Kate administered a local anaesthetic and watched as Angus drilled, then inserted a wide-bore cannula.

Working together, they set up a fluid line to keep the port open, and, while Angus watched for any change in their patient's condition, Kate continued her examination. The seat belt had left abrasions across the driver's chest and lap, and the depth and severity of them told her how violent the impact had been. Once in hospital, there'd be scans that would show the extent of the damage to the chest and abdomen.

Yet, even with possibly serious injuries, he was luckier than the people in the car. It had been dislodged from under the prime mover, and the damage told a grim story even before the firies started cutting out the bodies. Two people, driver and passenger, and neither had survived, which dampened the spirits of the SDR crew as they flew home with the rig driver.

Kate did the handover in one of the resus rooms in the ED, hoping they'd got the man to the hospital quickly enough to be saved, although she couldn't help wondering whether, if they'd flown him out earlier, his chances would have been better.

'You only do what you can,' came a voice from behind her as she left the hospital.

She knew before she turned that it was Angus.

'I'll walk you home,' he said, and because she was tired, not to mention doubtful about the outcome for her patient, she was hardly gracious.

'It's two blocks and broad daylight, I don't need to be walked home.'

'Ah, but my hotel is just across the road from your apartment building, and I might have been suggesting it because *I* needed to be walked home, only asking you to walk me home might have seemed a bit unmanly.'

Worried as she was, Kate had to smile. She turned to face him, taking in his height and breadth, and the aura of strength that hung around him, contrasting sharply with the gentleness in his dark eyes.

'Unmanly?' she echoed. 'That's not an assumption many people would make!'

He held out his arm, crooked at the elbow.

'So, shall we walk each other home?' he said, and somewhere deep inside a little bit of the Kate she used to be began to unfurl, like the petal on a tight rosebud. She slipped her hand inside his arm, telling herself it was just a friendly gesture, except that he cheated and turned his hand to grasp hers, linking them even closer together.

She should protest.

Move away!

But walking like this with Angus was warming places that had been cold for a very long time. Was it so very wrong to be enjoying it?

Well, probably, yes, given the secret she held so tightly in her heart.

But he'd be gone tomorrow, back to his own life, and she'd be back at work in Theatre and studying after hours, with exams drawing closer, so how could this little bit of closeness hurt?

He gave her hand a squeeze and because this was just for now, she squeezed back.

She pulled away from him as they reached the apartment block, intending to say a cool goodbye, but he caught her hand again, turning so he was facing her.

'Can I see you again?'

She shook her head.

'I don't think that's a good idea.'

He looked puzzled so, although he hadn't asked why not, she added, 'You're married, aren't you? You and Michelle? After all, that *was* what you went to island for—checking it out for a honeymoon.'

He smiled.

'I'd forgotten that's why I'd gone to the island—well, I hadn't thought about it for a while. No, we didn't marry.'

She waited, not wanting to ask why but aware he had more to say.

'She broke it off. I'd been away, came back changed, she said. And she was probably right. I *felt* different, less certain of things, not only between us but about life in general.'

Because of what had happened between us? Kate wondered, guilt biting deep inside her.

But before she could say anything, Angus was speaking again.

'And it didn't help telling her about you—about what had happened on the island.'

'You told her about the island? About the night we spent together? Oh, Angus, why on earth would you do that? It was one night. We were in another world—we knew it didn't mean anything but relief, or celebration, or something. I can't—' She looked up into his face as she said it, and saw that he still disagreed.

And understood.

His integrity would have insisted he tell, while she, Kate, had held onto her own secret, although it hadn't really been a secret until Angus had reappeared in her life.

And telling now? Wouldn't he feel the pain she'd felt? Those endless, sleepless nights and empty aching arms? Did he deserve that?

She shook away the thoughts and tried to ignore the cold, hard lump inside her.

'I need some sleep,' she said, and turned away from him, although she knew sleep would be impossible.

She made her way up to the apartment in a daze, ate some cereal—soggy—and toast—cold—and tried to pretend it had been just another callout.

'I'm sorry about the breakfast but I always get it ready when I hear the helicopter land,' Alice was explaining. 'Did you have a lot to do when you got back that you were late?'

Kate shook her head. The driver of the road train would have had a battery of tests and was probably getting appropriate treatment right now.

And the two young people, their lives cut short, were being taken by road transport to the nearest hospital.

'Bad, was it?' Alice asked, guessing from her silence that things hadn't gone well.

'Just about as bad as it gets,' Kate said, and then, knowing Alice would see or hear a report on a news broadcast, she added, 'It was a road train against a small car and the two young people in the car were killed.'

'That's shocking,' Alice said. 'So dreadful for their families.'

She paused, then added, 'But surely we should always take something from these terrible things—from such waste of life. Shouldn't it make us think about our own lives?'

Kate looked at the woman who had taken her in when she'd been at her lowest ebb and had coaxed her slowly back to at least a semblance of normal life.

'Do you have regrets about your life? Wish you'd done things differently?'

Alice smiled and shook her head.

'I'm talking about you, my dear. I know you're busy with your studies but life is meant to be lived, Kate. You should get out more, meet people away from your work. Those two had their lives taken from them, you still have yours and for their sakes, if nothing more, you should make the most of it.'

'And being the best surgeon I possibly can be isn't making the most of it?' Kate retorted.

Alice just shook her head and began to clear the table.

But Alice's words, perhaps because she so rarely talked about personal things and this was twice in two days, remained with Kate as she headed to her bedroom. And a hot shower failed to wash them away, so they lingered in her head, preventing any possibility of sleep. She heard the front door of the apartment open and shut and knew Alice had gone to help out at the charity shop down the road—Animal Welfare on Fridays. Alice's life was nothing if not predictable.

Giving up on sleep, Kate pulled on shorts and a light singlet. She'd go for a run, head out along the coastal path towards Coogee. Exercise and fresh, salty air would surely make her sleepy.

She enjoyed running, and today was even more special as the sun sparkled on the ocean while a gentle breeze kept her cool, and concentrating on where she put her feet and dodging walkers on the path kept her mind off both Angus's revelation and Alice's lecture.

She'd moved to the side of the path to allow a young woman jogging with a toddler in a stroller to pass in the opposite direction when she noticed the tall, upright figure striding—marching?—along the path in front of her.

Her heart flipped, and confusion fogged her mind—secrets, he's not married, another secret, her secret, and living life before it was too late all jumbled in her head.

And if she kept running she'd have to pass him.

Just run past?

Could she do that?

Not really!

Turn around and go back?

She usually ran as far as the huge cemetery, where sloping grounds gave such a wide view of the ocean, and to turn before that—well, it was hardly a run at all...

The memory of the young lives cut short sent her forward, slowing as she reached the marching man.

'Couldn't sleep?' she said, slowing to a jog

beside him. 'I couldn't either, but running always helps.'

He turned his head and looked at her for a moment, not breaking stride.

'The team should have had a debrief after an incident like that—after every incident, in fact.'

'We do, although today, because Blake went with the bodies to the nearest hospital, we'll have it later. Probably this evening. Mabel will let us know.'

'Jogging is bad for your knees and ankles,' he muttered, in an even more critical tone.

'I don't usually jog, I run,' she told him, curt to the point just short of rudeness because the man was causing so many strange reactions in her body. 'I'm jogging out of politeness to keep up with you, although you obviously don't want company, so I'll keep running.'

And she ran on, building up speed until she was running almost flat out by the time she reached her goal.

But even at full speed she couldn't outrun her awareness of Angus, stoically marching along the track behind her.

She settled on a grassy patch in the middle of the cemetery, beside a carved marble statue of a cherub that presided over the grave of a small boy who'd died back in 1892. His name had been Joshua and she'd been drawn to him although he'd lived for seven months, while her child, also a boy, had not lived at all.

And although her occasional chats with Joshua usually comforted her, today her thoughts were with her baby—Jasper she'd called him—and the way he'd felt in her arms as she'd held him that one time—

Had she been so lost in memories of that terrible day that she hadn't seen Angus approaching?

'Sorry I was grumpy,' he said, hovering above her. 'I couldn't sleep.'

He squatted down to read Joshua's memorial.

'I suppose parents in those days were aware their kids could die young,' he added, settling himself comfortably on the grass beside her as if it was the most natural thing in the world for them to be sharing this particular patch of grass.

Her patch of grass!

Hers and Jasper's…

'Do you think that would have lessened their grief?' she asked, handing him the water bottle she'd pulled from her small backpack, while certain she knew the answer to the question.

Nothing lessens grief like that...

He tipped his head back to drink and she saw the strong column of his neck, the slight bump of his Adam's apple, and added the images to others that she had of Angus, stored away safely in the back of her mind, only taken out to study on very rare occasions.

'No,' he said, startling her out of her dreams as he returned the bottle, his fingers brushing hers, confusing her body with the intimacy of a single touch.

'It could never be easy. I keep thinking of the families of those young people today. I've seen too many young people die, Kate, and the more I see, the more I think we owe them something. Owe it to them not to waste our own lives—to make the most of whatever time we have—not solely in pursuit of pleasure but both in work and play.'

Kate was silent for a moment, then admitted, 'Alice was saying much the same thing to me this morning. It was why I couldn't sleep.'

Was she saying what he thought she was?

Angus hesitated, wondering if he could put it to the test.

Nothing ventured, he reminded himself.

'So, if I asked very nicely, would you come to dinner with me?'

'Is that you asking, or asking if you can ask?'

She smiled as she said it and Angus took it as a small victory.

He laughed.

'I could say pretty please, but someone my size talking like that would be making a joke of it, and I'm not joking. I'd like to see you again, see you socially, nothing heavy or complicated, just a "'getting to know you" kind of arrangement.'

He wasn't really holding his breath, but studying the cherub on the grave gave him a chance to watch Kate's face more surreptitiously than staring at it. He could almost see the argument going on in her head, read it in the shadows in her eyes—more grey today—reflecting the sea?

'Okay,' she finally said, turning to face him, 'but it will be dependent on Blake and when he wants to do a debrief.'

She didn't smile and something about the set

of her face suggested she was pushing herself to accept.

Because she'd been a loner for a long time?

Because whatever had made her that way had left her scarred?

He was surprised to find that it hurt him to think of Kate hurting—scarred by something that had changed her so much.

'I'm flexible,' he said, 'and as I'd like to be part of the debrief we can make it before or after—whatever works.'

She stood up and stretched, her long, lightly tanned legs mesmerising him, her body reminding him—

Nothing heavy or complicated, he reminded himself.

'Are you walking on to Coogee?' she asked, and he shook his head.

'Then we might as well walk back together.'

Without waiting for a reply, she reached out a hand to pull him to his feet, and as he grasped it he wondered just how hard it would be to keep things light between them. Whatever magnetic force that had taken them to that dry bed in Cabin Thirty-Two—whispered to him by one of the staff as they saw the last of the injured and shocked guests off in the helicopter three years ago—was still alive and well between them. Or it was on his part, anyway.

The debrief, held late in the afternoon, eventually came to discuss whether the train driver should have been airlifted out immediately it was discovered there could be internal bleeding. The patient's falling blood pressure had suggested that scenario, and although holding onto him until they'd known the condition of the passengers in the car hadn't made any difference to his outcome, had the bleeding been worse, it could have been fatal.

Discussing it rationally, without the pressure of the emergency situation, was one of the ways they could improve their actions in the field, and was one of the important parts of the debrief.

'I think we were right to wait,' Kate said, although she'd been the one who'd asked for immediate evacuation. 'He was relatively stable and we had the IO line open if he'd needed massive doses of drugs or blood products. The ambulance attendants had started fluid resus and he had a distal pulse. The internal bleeding could have been from a tear to his carotid from the seat belt crossing his shoulder, or damage to an internal vein or artery from the lap-band of the seatbelt. There was no palpable swelling in his abdomen to suggest a lap-band tear and his trachea showed no signs of deviation so if there *was* bleeding from the carotid it wasn't affecting his airway.'

'Yet you suggested lifting him sooner?'

Kate smiled at Blake.

'Don't we always think the patient we're tending is the most important? Besides, it made minimal difference. The car was already out from under the road train and it was only a matter of minutes before you'd have ascertained if either of the occupants was alive. By the time we had Mr Grosvenor in the chopper you were able to tell us to take off.'

'Thankfully,' Blake said, and after a short general discussion the meeting broke up with Blake's usual reminder of the availability of a counsellor should any of them want to talk.

'Does he always beat himself up over what happened?' Angus asked as they walked out of the hospital.

'That wasn't exactly beating himself up,' Kate

protested. 'He's just determined that we should be the best we can, and it's only by going over the things we did—or sometimes didn't do—that we can improve.'

'But he *had* to hold the helicopter until he knew there were no survivors in the car,' Angus said. 'Anyone would.'

Kate stopped at the always open gates into the hospital and looked out over the shops and restaurants that lined the front to the ocean beyond.

'Are we going to continue to discuss this all through dinner?" she asked, and caught the surprise on Angus's face.

He held up his hands in mock surrender.

'Sorry, I get carried away.' There was a little pause before he half smiled and admitted, 'Actually, I'm incredibly nervous about this dinner.'

Kate grinned at him.

'Snap,' she said. 'I think the last time I felt this way was when I was fifteen and a boy I liked at school asked if I'd go to the pictures with him.'

'And did you?' Angus asked as they walked on. 'Go to the pictures with him?'

'I did,' Kate said, 'and we had popcorn and a milkshake and I got such a shock when he put his arm around my shoulders, I spilled the milkshake all over my dress. He did walk me home but he never asked me out again.'

'First dates!' Angus said, a small smile flirting around his lips.

'Tell me about yours,' Kate said, as they reached the promenade and turned to walk along it.

'Fifteen, and when I tried to kiss her, Michelle slapped my face.'

'Michelle?' Kate gasped. 'The Michelle you were going to marry? You went out with her from when you were fifteen?'

Guilt that she might have caused the breakup of such a long-standing relationship filled her chest, leaving her breathless as she waited for his reply.

'Why not?' Angus said, confirming Kate's worst fears.

'Well...'

What to say?

Did people still do that? Go out with each other exclusively from the age of fifteen?

'Did you go out with other people in between?' she asked, desperately hoping it had been an on-and-off relationship from the beginning.

'Off and on, both of us, but somehow we always ended up back together,' Angus said, sounding as unemotional as someone discussing the weather.

They'd been together fifteen years—she knew he'd been thirty when she'd met him—then had broken up after—

One night of madness…

Only it hadn't been madness, well, not to her. It had been as natural and necessary as the air she'd breathed.

The memory still felt that way.

But now the conversation, harmless as it had seemed at first, had erected a barrier between them, a wall of stupid, residual guilt as palpable as glass.

Angus wondered what she was thinking. They'd been chatting amiably enough and now even he, who wasn't always attuned to nuances in conversation or tension in the air, realised something had shifted.

Because he'd only ever seriously dated Michelle?

Surely not!

Time for a conversation change.

'Where's good to eat?' he asked, and when Kate looked blankly at him he added, 'Well, you're the local.'

'The bistro at the lifesavers' building,' she told him. 'There, on the rocks at the end of the beach.'

'The place beside the swimming pool in the rocks?'

'That's it,' she said, picking up speed as they headed towards it.

Escaping him or the conversation?

But the beauty of the night caught him, pushing away the awkwardness he'd felt. A pale half-moon had appeared just above the horizon, and its silvery light turned the unusually calm ocean into a sea of mercury.

'It's unbelievable—the beauty of the ocean,' he murmured, and she stopped and turned so they stood beside each other to admire the view.

'It is,' she said, and took his hand, squeezed

his fingers. 'Thank you for reminding me. Living here, it's easy to take it for granted.'

He looked down at her, at the dark hair that curled around her head like a cap, at neat brows and long eyelashes. Had she felt his gaze that she looked up, and her lips were right there?

He touched her cheek, lightly, and sensed her hesitation, then whatever it was that had flared between them on the island sent colour to her cheeks as she lifted her lips to meet his.

The kiss was slow, exploratory really, but it loosened something deep inside him that had been tight for a long time. Her lips were soft and warm against his, and her skin smelt of the beach, and sun, and flowers he couldn't name, and of a woman he'd kissed three years ago...

They turned and walked again, closer now, her hand in his, and the silence sat more easily between them.

But it didn't stop the doubts raging in Kate's head.

This was stupid, getting closer to Angus when all the physical stuff that had thrown them together once before was obviously still there between them...

The physical stuff that had led where it had...

It was only dinner!

And if dinner led to another dinner—even a date?

Led further?

How fair would that be, getting involved with him and not telling him.

She should tell him.

And just what would that achieve? Quite apart from the pain *she* could feel just thinking about talking about it, how would it affect him?

Wouldn't it hurt him too?

And if it didn't—

No, she couldn't tell him—couldn't talk about it—not without bringing up those traumatic days and the agony of grief that had followed them.

The pain that still hit her when she saw a small child—

'—heard a word I've said?'

She turned to the man who was causing her so much confusion.

'Sorry, miles away.'

And thinking unhappy thoughts, Angus decided, seeing sadness in her eyes as she'd looked up at him.

'Well, that's okay, because it wasn't very interesting chatter anyway,' he said, but her distraction reminded him of the 'loner' tag she had at the hospital. Wasn't that why he was hanging around Bondi? To see if he could find out what had changed her?

Not that it was any of his business, but he'd liked the Kate he'd met at the island, and maybe he could find her again beneath the shell she'd built around herself.

Oh, yes? a voice in his head taunted. *You want to see more of her for purely altruistic reasons? To find out why she's changed? Nothing to do with the attraction you feel towards her? The physical attraction you felt back then, that's still there between you? The attraction you'd like to follow up on? Have a bit of a fling?*

Except instinct told him that Kate wasn't a 'just a fling' kind of woman. A woman he could enjoy and walk away from.

Yet, if he'd hurt her in some way? If his actions had somehow contributed to the change in her personality, shouldn't he make an effort to sort things out?

And a fling would do that? that voice in his

head said mockingly, and he pushed all the useless thoughts away and concentrated on his guest.

'That rock pool looks fantastic. Someone was telling me there are people who swim here all year round.'

'Not me!' Kate assured him. 'I rarely go into the ocean until November when it's warmed up enough that I don't turn blue with cold.'

And just like that, things were easy between them again.

They were shown to a table by a window, far enough from other diners that they could talk freely, Kate asking him about his last posting, which he glossed over with a shrug and as few details as he could get away with.

Ordering dinner made a natural break in the conversation, so when that was done, he diverted the conversation back to her.

'And you?' he asked. 'Why surgery?'

For a moment, it seemed as if she might not answer, then she turned from the contemplation of the darkness beyond the window and looked directly at him, so he could see her face and read every expression on it.

'I liked the surgical work we did during training and then thought I'd follow up, but general surgery isn't as easy as it sounds and I'm determined to do well at it.'

'Why?' he asked again.

She frowned at him, although he was sure she knew full well what this question meant.

He leaned forward and touched one finger to her chin, a silent prompt.

'I wanted to do it for myself, to prove to myself I can be the best—or the best I can be.' She hesitated, then sighed as if she'd decided it was easier to get it all out than for him to keep prompting her. 'My parents were both high-fliers—lawyers—disappointed when I chose to study medicine instead of law. They'd wanted me to join the family firm, take it over in time. So, I felt I'd let the family down—failed.'

She looked out at the ocean again, remembering.

'I slightly redeemed myself by getting engaged to a lawyer then failed again by breaking off the engagement for what they felt was something trivial. Apparently, their marriage had survived many an affair! Other stuff happened, and I began to believe I *was* the way they saw me—a failure.'

She turned back to him, and he could read the determination in her face as she continued.

'I decided then I needed to do something for myself, something worthwhile that I could be good at, succeed at. Not for my family—I rarely hear from them now—but for myself. To regain my self-esteem.'

Angus studied this woman he knew but didn't know. There'd been a power in her words that told him they were true, but what could possibly have hit her so hard *she'd* believed herself a failure? Her family had started it, but the 'other stuff happened' was the real clue.

Would she tell him?

He reached out and grasped her hand. Gently squeezed her fingers, knowing he wanted her to, guessing she wouldn't.

CHAPTER THREE

'WHAT ARE YOU doing here?' Kate demanded, coming across Angus at the hospital gate the evening after their dinner.

'Waiting for you,' he said, giving her a peck on the cheek. 'Alice said you started work at seven so shouldn't be much later than seven coming home. What appalling hours.'

He'd linked his arm through hers and with her heart racing and her nerves tightening right through her body, she knew she should pull away—casually, of course.

But her arm didn't move, so she concentrated on the conversation, managing, she thought, to sound quite calm when she said, 'I'm often far later than this. I'm on call to the ED, and a patient who needs stitching invariably comes in as I'm sneaking off home.'

'That wouldn't have mattered,' Angus replied. 'I had the paper to read while I waited and that was only after I'd checked out the fish and chip shops. Fancy fish and chips on the beach?'

More fizzing going on inside her, which was just plain ridiculous!

Or was it?

Surely she could just enjoy the moment, whatever the moment might bring. Wasn't that what Alice had been trying to tell her?

'Sounds great,' she said, and relaxed, letting her body rest close to his as they walked down to the front and the fish and chip shop he'd chosen.

'Why this one?' she asked, although she knew it *was* the best.

'Longest queue,' he said, grinning at her in such a way her insides turned to mush.

'I should phone Alice,' she said as they waited at the end of the queue.

'Don't worry, I've already told her I was taking you out to dinner.'

'Fish and chips on the beach—you call that dinner?' Kate teased.

She was startled when he turned to her and said quite seriously, 'Well, I don't know how long I'll be able to hang around, so I can't waste too much time on the preliminaries.'

And just in case she hadn't caught his meaning, he kissed her lightly on the lips—a kiss that came and went so quickly she was left wondering if she'd imagined it.

Except that her body knew she hadn't. It had reacted with a quiver of excitement that brought her nipples to peaks and produced an ache of longing between her legs.

They inched forward in the queue, Angus chatting to the woman in front of them, Kate's mind in a whirl.

If he wasn't going to hang around, surely she could go along wherever this led, enjoy it while it lasted? And with a clear conscience about not telling him because it wasn't a 'relationship' but just a fling. And a flingee could have as many secrets as he or she liked, surely?

The idea of a fling, of seriously considering it, sent a tremor through her body, settling deep into the pit of her stomach, while a warmth began to envelop her.

Angus's arm brushed against hers, stirring up more chaos in her body, and strangely enough making her smile.

It would be fun, she realised.

Risky but fun.

A light touch on her arm…
Worth the risk…

They sat on a seat on the promenade to eat their dinner, not wanting sand in the chips, but after eating they took off their shoes to walk on the beach, hand in hand, replete, and content, for the moment, just to be together. But in the shadows at the far end, where the rocks began, he turned her so they faced each other, drew her close with his free hand, and this time kissed her properly.

His lips were hard and firm against hers, insistent, demanding, so her lips opened to him, his tongue invading the softness of her mouth, tasting her as she tasted him, teeth clashing as he dropped his shoes and used both arms to bind her tightly to him, her body pressed to his so she felt the shape and strength and heat of him, filling her with a need—an ache—to know more, feel more, be one with him.

And somewhere, in some still functioning part of her brain, she thought, This was what it was like the first time—this feeling of being truly alive—every cell of her body somehow recognising this man, wanting him, needing him, part of him somehow.

Heat built within her, consuming all thought, and she found herself responding with a passion she'd forgotten could exist.

'We have to talk,' he said when, needing to breathe, they finally drew apart.

It took a moment for Kate to register the words, but when she did the excitement drained from her body, leaving her cold and shaken.

We have to talk usually heralded something the listener didn't want to hear. And would his talking mean she had to talk…?

Tell…?

Angus had bent to retrieve his shoes, and now he slung an arm around her shoulders and steered her back along the beach, closer to the water now so little wavelets lapped across their feet.

But the silence was killing her, stretching as tight as a bowstring between them.

'So, talk,' she finally said, and he laughed.

'If only it was that easy.'

He paused, turning her again to face him, touching her hair, her cheek, his fingers outlining her lips.

'I think we're both adult enough to acknowledge the attraction between us, and I don't know about you, but I'd like to see more of you, enjoy some time with you—some special time.'

'You sound as if you're making a speech about your tent,' she told him, bemused by the delivery of his 'talk'.

He smiled and shook his head.

'This isn't easy, you know. In fact, it's damn near impossible. But what I'm trying to say is that whatever happens between us will be for now, can only be for now.'

His eyes grew serious.

'I don't want to make a big melodrama of it, but once I'm back on normal duty I won't know where I'll be from one day to the next. Most of my army mates have wives and families, and even though there are separations at times, it still works and works well. But now, possibly because I've been single, I've taken a different path. I've become involved with an emergency response unit and that led to designing and overseeing the manufacture of the prototype of what you rudely call "the tent" and some ancillary ones as well. But once it's

past the testing time in Australia and into production, then I'll have to go where they—the
tents—go. Can you see that?'

Earthquake zones, war zones, disease out-
breaks in developing countries—yes, Kate
could see each and every one of them, see them
all in terrible, horrific detail.

'So what we have is now,' she said softly, not
wanting to think beyond that, but at the same
time relieved because with 'now' the past didn't
matter.

Couldn't matter...

Then again, given how her body was reacting
to him, wouldn't this idea of 'just for now' leave
her wanting more or, worse, hurting again?

That was the risk.

But at least she'd feel alive again—and have
happy memories to take into the future.

How could it hurt?

Silly question—it had hurt before, hadn't it?

And back then she'd known that all they'd
have was just one night!

Except this time there'd be no consequence,
and that part had hurt the worst.

So why *not* just live for the moment—for
however many moments they might have?

Wasn't this just what she needed?

Something to jolt her out of the hole she'd dug for herself, to feel again—anticipation, excitement, desire, fulfilment—emotions she hadn't felt for so long…

He kissed her lightly on the lips, stopping all the arguments going on inside her head.

'The now,' he said, as they walked on. 'This isn't some great doom-laden thing, I'm pretty good at surviving anywhere, but it's the being away, the not knowing when I'll be back—it's destructive on relationships. I tried that with Michelle and it didn't work. It put too much pressure on her, far more than on me because I was always too busy to be thinking about anything but the minute, or hour, or day ahead.'

He paused as they walked up the steps, back to the promenade, then added, 'And I wouldn't like to do that to you.'

They sat again, Angus putting on his shoes, though Kate still held hers, the bottoms of her jeans so wet she was better without shoes.

'Well?' he said, when he'd tied his second lace.

Kate sighed.

'What am I supposed to say?' she asked.

'Back when I was dating—about a million years ago—we didn't have discussions like this. We went out a few times, kissed a few more, and if we both wanted to go to bed together, eventually we did. Or that's how it seems to have happened. Now it's like a timetable. If I say yes, will you tell me where to be and when so we can continue the whatever it is.'

He laughed and she added crossly, 'It's not funny!'

He leaned forward and kissed her on the lips, defusing the bit of what she'd felt was righteous anger, and bringing back all the sensations she'd been feeling… Was yearning the word?

'It's a little bit funny, you must admit, and hopefully fun,' he whispered against her lips. 'I just needed to be honest with you so you knew right from the start this wouldn't be a for ever and ever thing. I tried it once—well, more than once, but with the same woman—and it didn't work, so what do you think?'

He kissed her again before she could answer, not that she had an answer to give him, but somehow the kiss told her it would all work out, and made her admit that Alice had been right.

She'd shut herself away not only from others but from her own emotions for far too long.

It was time for a change!

'I'm on call tonight so I'm going home now,' she told him with only a little quaver in her voice. 'But now you've done your honesty thing, I should warn you that I work horrendous hours, and my work is just as important to me as yours is to you, so you'll have to put up with broken dates...'

She paused, looking at him.

'Will they be dates?' she asked, and he smiled at her, mischief glinting in his eyes.

'Oh, they'll be dates all right, just you wait and see.'

He stood up and put out his hand to help her to her feet.

'Come on, I'll walk you home and kiss you goodnight and you can text me your work schedule for the next few weeks or as long as you know it, and leave the rest to me.'

Kate chuckled.

'For such a good organiser you've forgotten one fairly important thing,' she told him. 'How can I text you when I don't know your number?'

He pulled her close and kissed her again, oblivious to the passers-by on the promenade.

'I'm glad you can still chuckle,' he said quietly as they drew apart, though not too far apart. 'That was something I remembered most about you.'

Angus gave her his card, pressing it into her hand, and felt her fingers close tightly over it—as if it was somehow precious—and for a moment he wondered if he was doing the right thing, seeing more of Kate while he was here. He'd made it clear to her that it was just, in her words, 'for now', but what of him?

Could he walk away so easily when this woman—and her chuckle—had not been far from his mind for the last three years?

But would it be fair not to?

In the darkened apartment entrance, he kissed her goodnight, holding her close, allowing a little of the emotion he was feeling to seep into the kiss.

Had she felt it that she responded, running her fingers up his neck to clasp his head with both her hands, and hold his lips to hers. It probably didn't go on for an aeon, but when she'd drawn away, then lightly pressed her lips to his with a whispered, 'Goodnight,' and he was walking back to his hotel, he felt as if it had lasted for ever.

Not that 'for ever' featured in his life these days.

From now on it was nothing more than 'for now'.

His mind was still in a pleasant haze, imagining what lay ahead, as he walked along the promenade towards the hospital late the next afternoon. His visit to the State Emergency Service headquarters had been productive, with positive comments about the little model of his tent—damn it all, she had him calling it that now! He'd taken notes of all the suggestions they'd offered, particularly in regard to some new fire-retardant spray under development. He'd have to follow up on that. The fabric of his tent was fire-retardant but no one had ever tested to what degree it would withstand fire and keep the workers safe inside it.

He'd made appointments for the next day, including one at a factory whose management had expressed interest in manufacturing the internal fittings for the tent—might as well stick to tent now—although the prototype was being made in Western Australia, and the real thing would probably be manufactured in China.

And he'd also made a booking at a restaurant up the hill behind the hospital that, he'd been assured, had a magnificent view of the beach. With Kate's roster saved on his cell-phone, he was confident that if her shift supposedly ended at five, she should be available for dinner by eight.

And about now, if she *did* finish on time, he'd be able to walk her home.

'Mickey!'

The frantic scream came from behind him at the same time as a small, tousle-headed boy flew past on a scooter, crashing full tilt into one of the recycling bins a careful council had placed along the promenade.

He reached the boy and bent to untangle him from the now buckled scooter, and saw the blood running copiously from a split lip.

If that was the only damage, he was lucky, Angus thought, feeling in his pocket for the clean handkerchief he'd folded in there that morning.

He was pressing it against the wound when

the mother arrived, and the child, getting over his initial shock, began to wail.

'He's okay, just a split lip,' he said to the mother. 'I'm Angus, I'm a doctor and I think it will need stitching. I can carry him up to the hospital—it will be faster than an ambulance.'

The mother half smiled, relief wiping some of the worry from her face.

'Are you sure?' she said, one arm around Mickey and the other hand holding the mangled scooter. 'He's got so big now I can barely lift him.'

'Quite sure,' Angus said, putting his arms around the little boy and lifting him as he stood up. 'Okay, Mickey?' he said. 'We'll get that lip of yours fixed in no time. I bet the other kids at kindy will be jealous when they see your stitches.'

Mickey stopped wailing while he thought about that, then recovered enough to say, 'School, I go to school. I'm a big boy now.'

'That's grand,' Angus told him as he strode towards the hospital, Mickey's mother trotting by his side. 'It's even better to go to school with stitches. And you'll have a great bruise to show your friends, all blue at first and maybe purple.'

'Or black?' Mickey asked hopefully. 'I like black.'

They were still discussing the colours of bruises when they reached the ED, where the first person he saw was Sam Braithwaite, Blake's fiancée, whom he'd met at the talk.

'Uh-oh,' she said, as she took him straight through to a small paediatric room. 'Looks like Kate's not getting off on time. We do minor stitches here but for a face, especially a child's face, we call for help.'

Kate felt a spurt of annoyance as her pager went off. She'd really thought she'd be leaving on time for once—secretly hoping Angus might be there to meet her. Putting on a bit of make-up and lipstick, and blushing as she did it, so out of touch with 'dating' she felt more trepidation than excitement.

She blotted off most of the lipstick, and hurried down to the ED.

Where Angus was dominating the space in the small theatre room.

'You're like a genie who pops out of a bottle, just appearing in front of me wherever I go,' she muttered at him.

Only not quietly enough, for the child—a small boy—on the table piped up. 'Genies come out of lamps, not bottles,' he told her, his voice muffled by a gauze pad he was holding to his upper lip.

'Angus rescued me and he's going to stay with me instead of Mum, 'cos Mum faints when she sees a needle, and if she's on the floor the stitching lady—is that you?—would have to walk around her all the time.'

'I see,' Kate said weakly, wondering just how Angus, Mum and the small boy had all come to be together. Apparently, they'd shared more than a few minutes because she could hear Angus in the boy's words.

'So, let's see what we've got,' she said, and lifted the pad. While Angus talked to the boy about the new scooter he'd have to get, Kate examined the wound.

'Whatever he'd hit must have had a sharp edge as it's a through and through cut, impacting on the inside of the mouth.' She smiled at the boy—Mickey Richards, she'd discovered from Angus's talk—and said, 'I'm going to have to stitch your lip, Mickey, but I'll give you something that will stop it hurting. We use what we call gas and you just breathe it in like you breathe in air and you might go into a dreamy sleep, but you won't feel a thing while I fix your lip.'

She turned to Sam, who'd followed her in to assist.

'Have you spoken to the mother? Explained we'll need to sedate him—?'

'And got her written permission,' Sam finished for her. 'And I know you like using nitrous oxide so I've got it ready. Nose mask and fifty-fifty with the oxygen?'

Kate checked the admission report with Mickey's weight and nodded.

'Now, Sam's going to put the mask over your nose and all you have to do is breathe through it for a few minutes.'

She paused.

'And no chatting to Angus while I'm stitching. I need your lip to stay still.'

But Mickey was already in a pleasant dream world and she doubted there'd be much chat.

She checked for any broken or cracked teeth. He'd been lucky as they were all intact.

Sam slid a suction device into his mouth, keeping it away from the wound. Kate flushed the tear, checking there were no tiny pieces of debris in it, then set to work.

She used absorbable sutures to fix the wound inside his mouth, knotting each stitch four times.

'Why the bigger knots?' Angus asked, peering into Mickey's mouth. Kate realised she'd been so caught up in her work she'd forgotten he was there.

Almost forgotten.

Except for little prickles on her skin.

And a slight flutter as she caught his deep voice saying something to Sam.

Concentrate on what you're doing!

But she still risked a glance at him as she answered.

'You know what it's like when there's something irritating in your mouth, a broken tooth, a tiny cut or graze?'

'You can't help poking it with your tongue,' he replied, and although she couldn't see him now as she *was* concentrating on her stitching, she knew there'd have been a smile on his face.

'Exactly!' she said, tucking the knots into the tissue under the repair to further safeguard them. 'Tying more knots stops them unravelling.'

'Do you use absorbable sutures on the outer skin as well?'' Angus asked, and Kate nodded.

Medical chat made things easier.

'They're best on young kids as it saves them the added trauma of having to have them removed. The outer layer is trickier as we need to align the vermilion, that white line around the lips, or the scar will show.'

She worked quickly but carefully, smiling ruefully to herself as she realised Angus would know as well as she did what the vermilion was.

Angus.

She'd finished and as she wiped small spots of remaining blood from Mickey's face, she allowed herself to again give in to her awareness of Angus's presence.

As a man.

Her man!

Well, her 'for now' man anyway...

Sam brought Mickey's mother into the room to be with him as he rested, a dreamy smile on his face.

'Did I go to sleep?' he asked Angus.

'Maybe dozed, sport, and now you've got a new lip, want to see?'

He found a mirror and held it up so Mickey could see the repair.

'Cool!' the kid said, with a slightly lopsided smile.

'He's so good with children,' Mrs Richards said, and Kate's heart clenched in her chest.

He *had* been good with Mickey.

She put two small strip dressings on the repaired skin above his lip, then turned away to write a script for antibiotics, giving it to Mrs Richards and explaining she could get them at the hospital pharmacy or from her local chemist.

'Can I go now?' Mickey asked, obviously anxious to be gone so he could show off his stitches to all his friends.

'In a little while,' Kate said, touching him lightly on the shoulder. 'I'd like you to stay here and rest for a few minutes. See the clock on the wall? When the big hand gets to the nine you can go. Do you know your numbers?'

'Of course,' her patient told her in a tone of great disgust. 'I'm five.'

'And a very sleepy five,' his mother said, running her hand over his forehead as his eyes closed.

Leaving Sam to watch the child, she walked out with Mrs Richards, introducing herself properly and explaining that Mickey would probably be sleepy when he got home, and not to be concerned if he didn't want anything to eat, but some jelly or an electrolyte ice block would be good.

'See he keeps up his fluids and if he's in pain, he can have some children's paracetamol. If you're worried about anything, contact the hospital. There'll be someone who can talk to you.'

Voices from inside the room told them Mickey was ready to go.

'Can I see my scooter?' he asked as the two women returned.

'I put it in the bin,' Mrs Richards told him. 'It was all broken and we'll get you a new one just as soon as your lip's better.'

'Only you'll have to learn how to stop it,' Angus said, and Mickey laughed.

I could go now, should go now, Kate thought as Angus, Mickey and Mrs Richards chatted about scooters. One of the duty doctors will discharge him.

But she stayed until Mr Richards, apparently summoned by his wife, arrived to take his family home.

Kate followed them out the door, only too aware of Angus, who'd stopped to speak to Sam, just a few steps behind her.

Aware too of an inner unease that she'd felt since she'd first seen Angus with the child.

Unease she couldn't quite define, not sadness—or perhaps a little of that—but more what-ifs.

'You were terrific with that little boy,' she said to him as he drew up beside her. Saying something—anything—helped to hide all the physical manifestations of being near him that were now becoming common.

At least they'd chased away the unease…

'I like kids,' he said. 'I'd have liked to have some but Michelle felt, with me away so much, it might not be fair on them. I had to agree with her, but still…'

Michelle's name acted like a bucket of cold water on Kate's too-sensitised skin. Or had it been his talk of not having a child?

Practically blinded by the muddle of emotions churning inside her, Kate paused in the bustling hospital vestibule.

'I need to go back—get my things,' she said, and fled.

This was madness!

She was rushing into something because her hormones were in chaos, nothing more.

Except there *was* something more—something to do with feeling alive again, feeling at one with another human being, and wanting to share, to talk and laugh and, yes, make love.

Oh, yes, that was definitely part of it.

But she couldn't go into it—whatever it might be—with doubts or second thoughts. *Wouldn't* go into it that way!

She smiled to herself as excitement built within her once again. It might be just for now, but this was going to be a now she'd remember for the rest of her life…

Angus frowned as he watched her go. He'd been congratulating himself on being able to talk and joke with Mickey and his mother when all he'd really wanted to do was watch Kate. Not so much watch her stitch a cut lip but just watch her, wonder at the fate that had brought them back together, really look at her to see if he could understand just what it was that attracted him to her—or was it her to him—so strongly.

He tried to make sense of it as he walked out of the hospital, certain Kate would eventually exit but probably through some staff door he hadn't yet discovered.

She was smart—clever—and he liked that, and driven to succeed—a trait he shared—but that was mind stuff. What really puzzled him was the body stuff. He was sure his heart had probably skipped a beat when he's seen Michelle way back when they'd begun to go out together, but not every time he'd seem her, more when they'd been parted for a while.

With Kate, the little skip was there not only when he saw her but when he heard her voice, or thought about her agreeing to a short-term relationship.

For now, as she'd called it.

For a moment, he wondered if it had to be 'for now', the thought startling him so much he stopped mid-stride. No, the army was his life—well, not so much the army but definitely the tent. He wanted to see it through.

But if he *wasn't* in the army?
He pushed the thought away…

CHAPTER FOUR

KATE HAD A quick shower in the staffroom, washing her hair, which always seemed to smell of disinfectant after even a small procedure at the hospital. She towelled it dry, pulled on the clean undies she kept in her locker, then studied the other clean clothes stashed in it. They weren't up to much, apart from being clean—jeans, a T-shirt, an ancient parka in case it was cold walking home, and…

On a hanger, right at the back, a pair of black slacks and a dark blue cotton-knit sweater that she'd brought along one night when the SDR team were going out to dinner to celebrate something she could no longer remember.

She'd been held up in Theatre so hadn't gone, but the clothes had stayed in her locker. They'd have to do, although a little bit of her wished she'd had something to dress up in to go out on this 'date'.

Not that she had much that counted as dressy

at home either. Alice had been right. She'd shut herself away for far too long.

Not any more!

Hurrying now, she dressed, applied minimal make-up—a little mascara to her eyes and bright red lipstick—and set off to meet Angus again.

For a date!

Her heart skittered and she paused to wonder if it was normal for a woman of her age to be feeling so—so what? Nervous certainly, yet excited. Upbeat, yet worried about what she might be flinging herself into.

Then the thought of Angus brought warmth rushing through her body, and a glint to the eyes she could see in the mirror.

You only have one life, she reminded herself, thinking of Alice's words after the accident.

So go live it! she told her reflection, and all but marched out of the hospital.

'Nice transformation,' Angus said as he met her, but it was the admiration in his eyes that was her reward. She smiled at him, more at ease now.

They walked up the hill to the restaurant, a

light sea breeze teasing Kate's hair, Angus's deep voice teasing other bits of her.

How far would a 'for now' relationship go?

How far did she want it to go?

A different stirring inside her now, giving her an answer, so when Angus linked his arm through hers, she let him draw her close and sensations as powerful as a kiss flooded through her.

And through him, that he drew her into the deep shadows of an overhanging tree and kissed her hard and long?

Her legs were shaking as she drew away, desire flaming through her, heating her body, sensitising her nipples.

'I can cancel our reservation,' he whispered, telling her he'd felt it too.

'I guess we have to eat,' she said, denying the new surge of emotion.

'I guess we do, but perhaps…'

They'd reached the restaurant and hesitated in the light outside it, and the matching heat of desire in Angus's eyes all but stole her breath.

'One course,' she said softly. 'And a glass of wine, not a bottle.'

He grinned, devilment dancing in his dark eyes.

'And all the time I'll be thinking what we'll do—what I'd like to do to you and like you to do to me.'

Kate felt the heat flare in her cheeks.

'Perhaps we should have cancelled,' she murmured, the huskiness of her voice a dead give-away of her feelings.

Alex took her elbow and swept her up the steps.

'Come on, I've booked a table with the best view of the beach.'

The waiter showed them through onto a small balcony, and Kate could only shake her head.

'It's beautiful! I've seen the suburb at night but never like this,' she said.

"So glad m'lady approves,' Angus said, doffing an imaginary hat and bowing low.

Blushing again, Kate sank into the chair the waiter was holding then breathed in the fresh sea air.

Things were moving far too fast for someone who'd been a loner for two—three really—years. Yet she wanted this man in a way she'd never felt before—wanted to be in bed with him, hot and hard and urgent in her need.

'What?' she demanded, turning back to see him smiling at her.

'You could never play poker,' he teased.

'Why not?' she asked, and he laughed.

'Every thought you have is written on your face, every doubt is shadowed in your eyes.' And, still smiling added, 'I won't rush you into this, Kate.'

This time any colour in her cheeks would be from embarrassment, but she didn't have the words for her unease. Perusing the menu took a bit of time, and ordering a little more, but when that was done Angus reached across the table and took her hand.

'What's bothering you?'

She smiled, partly because his holding her hand was very nice indeed but also because it was easy to talk to Angus.

'Every single thing about this whatever it is— not the actual getting together bit of it, or even the "for now" part, but I suppose it's because we don't really know each other, do we, yet later tonight we'll probably be in bed—'

This time his grin sent goose-bumps down her spine.

'Getting to know each other better,' he pointed out, and she gave up.

She'd tuck all doubts—particularly about secrets—deep down in her heart, and go with the flow, see where it led, knowing it would end when the army sent him somewhere—tomorrow, or next week, or, with any luck, maybe in a month.

Or two?

Now you're being greedy, she chided herself, removing her hand from Angus's grip as their meals arrived.

They talked of Mickey and his mother, which led to childhood accidents.

'I fell out of a tree when I was six,' Angus told her. 'Mum saw me lying on the ground and fainted, which was helpful. Fortunately, a neighbour had heard me yell and came rushing in. He called an ambulance and they thought it was for Mum, who was still lying on the ground, so no one took much notice of my broken arm until they'd made sure Mum was all right and had driven away.'

'So, what happened then?' Kate asked, mainly

to divert her mind from picturing Angus as a young boy.

'Oh, the neighbour drove me to hospital. I think he fancied Mum but she never looked twice at him. Or at any man after my dad died. He'd been in the army and was killed in a helicopter crash—not shot down in anger, just a chance malfunction of some kind back at home.'

'That's terrible,' Kate said, and he shook his head.

'It was for Mum but I didn't really remember him. I was barely two so my memories are from photos of him in his army uniform.'

'And your mother?'

'Died when I was ten. The official word was cancer, but Gran, who brought me up, with a bit of help from a couple of uncles, always said it was grief.'

It was Kate's turn to reach across the table to touch Angus's hand, but although he squeezed her fingers in response, he wouldn't accept sympathy.

'Don't feel sorry for me, I had a perfectly happy childhood. Gran was fantastic. One of my uncles is a doctor and so I chose the army for my father and a doctor because of him, which got me to where I am today.'

'But losing your mother like that,' Kate murmured.

Angus shrugged, broad shoulders rising.

'Mum was sick for a long time so Gran had always been my rock—'

He paused, looking at the woman across the table—the woman he barely knew yet felt he knew.

'A bit like Alice was yours, I imagine,' he finished, and was pleased when Kate smiled.

'Only too true,' she said, pushing her empty plate away. 'Shall we go?'

As a hunger unlike any he'd ever felt before had been gnawing away at his intestines since she'd walked out of the hospital—slim and upright, the blue top thing she wore making her eyes seem bluer—he didn't argue.

He gave the waiter his card, signed the bill and, as quickly as decency allowed, led her out of the restaurant.

'Should you phone Alice?' he asked.

She leaned into him, kissed his cheek.

'Did it from the hospital—told her not to wait

up. But I'll have to go home sometime, I'm on an early shift.'

'Then off for three days, is that right?'

She chuckled, a soft warm sound that sounded like small bells in his ears.

Small bells in his ears?

What was that about?

'Yes, three whole days,' she was saying when he'd pulled himself together.

'Shall we go away?'

She turned to face him, obviously puzzled.

'Go away?' she echoed.

'Yes,' he said, 'together, somewhere nice—well, different—just the two of us. To Sydney maybe.'

'We're already in Sydney,' she pointed out as he steered her back down the street.

'But right in Sydney, in the city, a big anonymous hotel, do the sights, Luna Park, the Zoo, ferry rides to Manly or up the river. Let me show you my home town. There's more to Sydney than Bondi Beach, you know.'

'Hush your mouth,' she said, laughing as she spoke. 'Don't let anyone around here hear you say that!'

So they were both laughing when they

reached his hotel, and although he could feel her body, close beside his, grow tense as they walked in, she didn't falter, standing beside him while he got his key and following him to the elevator, his hand now clenched in hers.

'Hey,' he said softly, using his forefinger to tilt her head to his as the elevator rose, 'we don't *have* to do this, you know.'

The ping told them they'd arrived, and he put his arm around her shoulders and steered her down the hall to his door.

But once inside he held her lightly in the circle of his arms, face to face.

'I like you, Kate, and I'm attracted to you, and I'd like to get to know you better—both in bed and out. It's not just about the sex so if you're not comfortable with it just tell me.'

He dropped a light kiss on her lips and waited.

'I suppos—' she began. 'I don't—'

She hesitated again. 'Oh, damn it all!' she finally said. 'Just kiss me, Angus. I don't want to analyse it all.'

He did as he was told and kissed her, and she kissed him back, which led eventually to a frantic shedding of clothes before they fell on the bed, wanting each other but prolonging it, learning each other's shape and textures, teasing, heightening the pleasure until neither of them could wait any longer.

Kate must have dozed and she woke in Angus's arms, filled with a peace and contentment she hadn't felt for a long time.

Would she wake him if she moved?

Was not waking him enough of an excuse to stay?

She smiled to herself and ran her free hand along the arm that held her, up to his shoulder, warm, and hard with muscle.

Sneaked a finger further along to touch his cheek, his straight nose, his close-cut hair.

Would the ba—?

She pushed the thought away, far away, back down into the bottom of her heart.

She was with Angus here and now and the past would stay the past...

And she had to leave—had to get home, grab a couple of hours' proper sleep and get to work.

Reluctantly she eased her way out of the warm comfort of his arm, away from the treacherously tempting body that had filled her with such delight.

He slept on. An army thing, she imagined, grabbing sleep when it was available because who knew when they'd need to not only be awake but aware with every sense of the enemy around them.

She scrabbled around the room, finding her hastily shed clothes and pulling them on, raking her fingers through her hair, aware that walking out of the hotel at two in the morning was going to be highly embarrassing.

But well worth it, she decided as she crossed the road to her apartment block and crept silently into her own bed where she could close her eyes and remember—relive the sensations—as she fell asleep.

But when the alarm woke her, what seemed only minutes later, she tucked all the memories and sensations away in a new box in her mind—the 'for now' box—and concentrated on what might lie ahead of her when she reached the hospital.

She'd barely shut her handbag away in her locker when her pager summoned her back to the ED. One of the young doctors on duty apologised as he explained.

'She's not entirely sober and she fell through

a glass coffee table. Eight-inch gash on her upper right arm and other minor injuries. We've flushed the arm wound. Apparently, the table broke cleanly into three pieces, rather than shattering.'

He led the way into the suture room where a large woman in tight jeans and a red bra was sitting on an examination couch, crying quietly. A nurse was holding a pad to the injured arm, and the local anaesthetic and sutures Kate would need were laid out on a tray at the side of the room.

'So silly,' the woman said to her new audience. 'I was fighting with my boyfriend—just yelling, not pushing and shoving kind of fighting, and he made me so mad I stormed across the room and, bang, there I was with the table broken all around me.'

She paused, peering over her shoulder to watch Kate take the dressing from her arm.

'Now he's going to be really angry because he loved that table. He didn't even bring me to the hospital, just phoned for an ambulance and it took for ever and now I'm going to have a great ugly scar down my arm—'

'We'll try to make sure it isn't a great ugly

scar,' Kate said quietly, pleased to see the wound, though deep in parts, hadn't damaged any major blood vessels.

Her brain was racing. She understood why the staff here had called her, rather than send the woman up to Theatre. According to the chart, she'd eaten a full dinner at about ten the previous night and been drinking wine and nibbling on cheese and biscuits until shortly before she'd fallen, so she couldn't have a full anaesthetic.

Not that the wound necessitated that, but with the alcohol in her, she needed to be sedated. A mild dose of ketamine, easy to administer into a muscle and safe to use on inebriated patients. She spoke to the nurse, who hurried away to get the drug, while Kate checked the sutures on the tray.

Some internal absorbable ones for the inner layer of skin on the deeper part of the wound, and exactly what she'd have chosen for the closure.

She smiled to herself, aware she shouldn't be surprised. She'd spent a lot of time in the ED, sewing up injured patients, and most of the staff knew how she worked. And conscious of not leaving a bad scar, she worked carefully, although it meant she was going to be late for assisting in a scheduled op with her supervisor.

Not that he'd need her—it was an op an intern could assist with, but she admired the man who was guiding her career path at the moment, and loved watching him work.

Slipping late into Theatre, the nod her supervisor gave her acknowledged that he'd known where she'd been, but settling into her accustomed place across the table from him was—

Well, different somehow.

As if!

Surely one night of romance didn't mean everything had changed.

So why did it feel that way?

She looked around but all the faces were familiar, so she glanced up into the glassed-in gallery above the theatre—the usual bunch of students there, some in white coats, some in civvies.

Some in civvies?

She darted another look into the gallery.

No, she hadn't been mistaken, that was definitely Angus up there, talking to one of the hospital administrators, a new man she'd heard of but had rarely seen.

She forced herself to concentrate on what was happening in front of her, steeling herself against the silly flutters in her body, focussing on cauterising small bleeders, holding organs out of the surgeon's way, taking over the closing of the wound, slowly and carefully, not daring to look up but hoping he was gone.

Or that maybe he'd been an apparition!

She went straight from Theatre to the side room, where she stripped off her scrubs and tossed them into a bin before showering and changing back into clean ones. One of the gynaecology surgeons was doing a keyhole removal of an ovarian cyst, and she wanted to watch the screen as he worked through a tiny slit—well, three tiny slits.

The ever-expanding use of keyhole surgery fascinated her and although she'd only ever used it to clear infection from an injured knuckle joint—under the watchful eye of a hand surgeon—she wanted to learn as much as she could of the different uses to which it could be put.

Or was this rushing to another theatre more to

do with avoiding the possibility of meeting the apparition in the corridor? It probably hadn't been him, although her skin had thought it was. But what could he possibly be doing here, and how could she concentrate on work if he was going to keep popping up all over the hospital? She didn't care whether genies came out of bottles or lamps, there was definitely something genie-like about his appearances in front of her.

Not to mention distracting!

Angus had been surprised when his uncle had suggested they look in on an operation. He'd imagined that, as an administrator, his uncle would sit in an office all day.

Waking to find Kate gone, the day had seemed to stretch endlessly in front of him. The phone call from his uncle had also surprised him as the last time he'd seen him, the man who'd been his role model as a child had been working at Royal North Shore Hospital on the other side of the city.

Apparently, increasing difficulties with the arthritis that had plagued him for years had led him to consider administration—and Bondi Bayside had needed just such a person.

'Word reached me that you were about,' he'd said, then invited Angus to meet him at the hospital. 'I've got a bit of administrative stuff to do, then we'll have lunch.'

The 'administrative stuff' had taken them to one of the theatres and it had to have been fate that Kate had walked into the tableau below the viewing balcony. Even in a blue bandana and oversized blue scrubs she had looked beautiful to him, and his body had tightened just looking at her.

Had she seen him when she'd glanced up?

He couldn't tell, although he could almost feel her concentration as she avoided looking up again...

'Are you with me or off somewhere in that busy head of yours?' his uncle asked as he led him into the admin lunch room.

It was a question his uncle had often asked the child who'd been Angus, usually in the middle of a 'little talk' about the world and its ways. Angus had invariably stopped listening, his attention caught by a butterfly alighting on a flower, or a passing bus if they'd been in the city.

'Sorry,' he said. 'I was diverted.'

'By a woman, I hope, or thoughts of one. It's time you were married.'

'Aah!'

It was an old conversation. His family had known and liked Michelle but although that was over, as far as this uncle was concerned, it was a man's duty to get married and have children.

But Angus had the perfect diversion for him.

'I was actually wondering what it would be like working in a hospital if I left the army,' he said, because this was another of his uncle's favourite topics.

'Well, I could put in a word for you at North Shore, or I'm sure there'd always be a job for you here,' he said. 'Actually, one of the doctors on our Specialist Disaster Response team has recently left, and you'd fit right in there.'

Which led to talk of his trip out with the SDR and the development of his tent and the subject of marriage was forgotten.

But the marriage idea stayed in his head, and it was only by reminding himself of the dangerous positions he'd been in in the past that he was able to banish it.

He turned his thoughts to where to stay in

Sydney. Harbour views, not too far from the city centre, close to Centennial Park for walks. He'd grown up in Balmain, near enough to the city to know it well, and although the army had taken him far and wide, Sydney would always be home to him.

Somehow, Kate got through the day. The apparition hadn't helped but by the time she left work, on time for once, she'd convinced herself she'd been seeing things—memories of the night before sending false messages to her brain.

But as she was leaving the hospital, the sight of a tall, well-built man leaning into the window of a rather posh car, and the skip of a heartbeat, suggested she hadn't been mistaken.

The car was leaving the executives' car park.

And for one, probably foolish, moment she allowed herself to imagine Angus had been at the hospital enquiring about a job—thinking of leaving the army.

By the time he'd straightened and given the top of the car a tap, she'd remembered the tent and his passion for it—his determination to eventually provide the best possible facilities for teams sent into disaster areas.

And to be there to see that they got it!

Of course he wouldn't leave the army…

She sighed, remembering too that this was just for now…

He turned as the car drove away, saw her and strode towards her.

'Just found out my uncle—the doctor one—is one of your bosses. It's hard to keep up with me moving around all the time and him being so busy. Last time I heard from him he was on the other side of the harbour. He'd heard I was around and asked me to lunch.'

He'd put his arm around her and dropped a kiss on the top of her head as he spoke, causing such a riot of sensations in Kate's body she barely made sense of the words.

'Saw you in Theatre, too,' he continued, steering her onto the footpath, his arm still clamped around her waist. 'Wanted to wave but didn't want to distract you.'

Kate stopped, which pulled him up quite sharply. He looked down at her and smiled.

'Talking too much?' he asked. 'I'm just so

glad to see you, and I've been thinking about the fact we'll have three whole days together.'

She saw the gleam of excitement in his dark eyes and felt a shiver of anticipation.

'You okay to leave tonight? It's not too soon? Will it be all right with Alice?'

'Tonight? We're going tonight?'

Was it too soon? Was she ready for this? Had she even said she'd go? And did she really want to spend three days with this man who, considered realistically, she barely knew?

Except she did know him—knew he was great in a crisis, knew he was kind and considerate, knew, too, that he was honest, that this would be just what it was—something for now.

And he was patient, too, she realised, for he was just standing there, waiting for her answer, not asking again or persuading her.

But just looking at him her body throbbed with excitement.

No, it wasn't too soon and, yes, she *was* ready!

So why not tonight?

'Alice will be delighted,' she told him, and they turned to walk again.

But packing proved a more difficult task than

talking about it. She dithered in her bedroom while Angus chatted to Alice as if he'd known her for ever, his ease with older people no doubt coming from growing up with his grandmother.

Just stop thinking tangential thoughts and pack.

But what?

September in Sydney meant warm sunny days but cooler nights, and who knew when a westerly wind would blow in at any moment and turn the city into an ice-box.

A very windy ice-box.

She put in slacks, three summery tops, a jacket for the evenings, and would take a parka just in case the wind did come.

But, oh, why was all her underwear so practical, so predictable? White bras and knickers, black bras and knickers, not a bit of lace or pretty ribbon anywhere.

If they didn't go tonight she could make a dash to Bondi Junction and…

And tell Angus what?

That you can't go tonight because you don't have pretty underwear? From what she was getting to know of the man, he'd insist on taking her to a lingerie shop first thing in the morning and probably make her parade in front of him for his approval.

More for his amusement as he'd know she'd be embarrassed.

She paused, cotton knickers in hand, as a thrill ran through her. Was this really happening? Was she about to take an enormous leap out of her self-imposed isolation—out of the safe little world she'd made for herself—into the arms of a man she barely knew?

Except she *did* know him in ways it might take a lifetime for other people to know each other. The fraught hours when they'd hidden their own fears to care for the terrified tourists and even staff on the island had formed a bond between them that she knew, meeting him again, was still there.

Damn it all, underwear was underwear, and she doubted she'd be standing around in it for long. He'd managed to get it off her very expertly the previous evening.

She threw in the underwear, toiletries and make-up, a squashy hat and some good walking shoes, and was done.

Quick shower and they could go, although Alice had probably already regaled him with all the mishaps of her youth and the disaster of her non-wedding!

Night had fallen by the time they'd checked in at the hotel and reached their room. As the door closed behind the porter, Angus put his arm around her shoulders and led her to the windows.

'It's breathtaking,' she whispered, awed by the spread of beauty before her. The twin trails of red and white lights as cars crossed the Harbour Bridge, the well-lit ferries carrying commuters home from work and bringing people back to play in the city, and closer, just beneath them, the city itself, neon lights pulsing and strobing, as if in time to the heartbeat of the city.

Angus had raided the mini-bar and opened a half-bottle of champagne, handing her a glass as she stared in wonder at the view.

'Just a glass now because we've a big night ahead of us,' he said, but when he put his arm around her the hunger she'd felt earlier returned and as the light kiss he dropped on her lips became hard and demanding, she knew his plans for the evening would have to be delayed.

* * *

'We can't go on like this for three days,' she said some time later, sitting up in bed, finishing her warm and flat champagne. 'I'll be too exhausted to go back to work.'

Angus was lying behind her, running one finger slowly down her spine, as if counting her vertebrae, making sure they were all there.

'Angus?' she said, thinking his finger might be moving in his sleep, but he'd reached the small of her back and flattened his hand against her skin, curling it around her waist and effortlessly easing her back down beside him so they lay face to face.

She studied him, this man who had almost literally swept her off her feet. What was it about him? What made him different? Surely it had to be more than body chemistry.

There was his kindness—she'd seen that with Mickey. And in the way he chatted to Alice, showing a genuine interest in her charity work.

And his passion for his work—that ran deep within him.

Then—

Her brain stopped working as his finger

traced her face, and the lips she'd been watching spread in a small, satisfied smile.

'Don't look so smug,' she told him. 'I'm here because I want to be, not because you're some irresistible lover.'

'Ah, but I am to you, aren't I?' he said, tracing her lips now and slowly awakening all the feelings that had led them to this position.

'Yes,' she admitted. 'It's the why that's got me puzzled.'

He leant up on one elbow and leaned over to kiss her.

'Don't overthink it, just enjoy it.' He sat up, all business now. 'So, do we go out to eat or order room service?'

'I love room service when I stay in hotels, especially at conferences and seminars,' she admitted.

'That's because you've become antisocial— I've been around the hospital and staff often enough to have picked that up—and someday you'll tell me why but I think probably a little bit of fresh air would do us both good so let's shower and get some clothes on and see what this wonderful city has to offer us in the way of a meal.'

The shower took longer than expected but eventually they were dressed and out on the street, wandering hand in hand among the bustling streams of people who never seemed to leave city streets.

'Ha!' Angus suddenly declared, halting their aimless meander. 'I wondered if it was still here. You like Moroccan food?'

'Love it,' Kate assured him. 'It's something I like to cook, so I'm sure I'll find plenty of new dishes to try.'

The restaurant was richly decorated with carpets, intricately carved panels and filmy curtains, draped to provide private spaces for the diners. Low, satin-covered sofas and huge cushions provided the seating and candles burned in ornate silver holders, sending a faint, musky scent into the air.

'Have you been there, Morocco?' Kate asked when they were seated.

'Once—a flying visit. Unfortunately, I missed all the colour and splendour of the architecture and saw a lot of desert. Famine in the Western Sahara had brought a horde of refugees flooding across the border, many of them with diseases we rarely see, like malaria, cholera and

Hep A. I was in Stockholm at the time, they do a lot of disaster response work, so I went with their team to do what we could to help those who were sick, but mainly to set up water purification plants.'

Kate smiled and shook her head.

'Stockholm and Morocco,' she said. 'Both sound equally exotic to me.'

'But you could travel—you get well paid. At least you could take holidays in some of these places.'

Her smile faded as she realised just how limited her life had become.

'I've just never thought about it,' she admitted. 'I suppose it was the thought of doing it alone—not having anyone to turn to, to remark on the beauty or wonder or something in particular and no one to share the memories with afterwards.'

Angus hoped the frown he was feeling inside wasn't showing on the outside. Admittedly, back on the island, he hadn't known Kate well, but he was absolutely certain that that Kate would have at least *considered* foreign holidays. And she'd been quite happy—well, maybe not *happy* happy but content somehow—when she'd honeymooned alone...

In fact, he remembered talking to her about far-off lands during the night they'd sat out the cyclone. Travel had definitely been in her future.

So, what had happened that had made her turn in on herself, as if curling herself around some hidden hurt?

Would he eventually find out?

He couldn't ask—at least, he didn't want to ask. Deep inside he was hoping she'd trust him enough to tell him.

Eventually?

Except there wouldn't be an eventually.

Couldn't be one. Not with the lifestyle he led, and would be leading for the foreseeable future.

He shook away his thoughts, glad Kate had been diverted by the description of the dishes on the menu while he'd brooded. While he'd realised, with a definite shock, that the last thing he should be considering was an 'eventually' together!

'Listen to this,' she said, turning to him with a smile. 'It sounds like an Indian biryani, which has layers of rice and meat, only this one has couscous in place of the rice and the meat has apricots and dates through it.'

She read out the description and as he watched the animation in her face he—

What?

Forget it!

This is for the here and now, remember. Tomorrow you could be anywhere.

He ordered the dish she'd talked about, and distracted his wayward thoughts in a discussion with the wine waiter. A nice rosé should do the trick, they decided.

He turned back to Kate, caught her perusing him in much the same manner he'd been watching her with the menu earlier.

'It's kind of exciting, getting to know someone new,' she said, adding with a smile, 'Well, almost new.'

The smile made his bones melt.

Men's bones didn't melt!

Not soldiers' bones anyway.

Shouldn't have had the champagne.

'It is,' he said, smiling back. See, it's easy being normal.

Except if this was normal he was in trouble...

* * *

Angus seemed a little distracted, but Kate was so entranced by the décor and the menu she was happy to carry the conversation, pointing out carpets she particularly liked, or reading the ingredients of dishes she'd like to try at home.

'You could come for dinner one night and I'd cook it,' she said, and although Angus smiled and accepted the offer politely, she knew something had shifted between them.

Maybe not between them, but on his side anyway.

Was her inviting him to dinner a step too far from their 'here and now' relationship?

She shook away the thought. They had three days together, that was the here and now, and she was going to enjoy every minute of it.

No doubts, no regrets, no analysing their relationship, because there really wasn't one. And when it finished, at least she'd have good memories this time, memories of fun and laughter, and of simply being together.

They rode the ferry to Manly the next day—the old ferry, not the fast commuter—and Kate marvelled at the number of little bays and inlets on either side of the harbour, many with houses right down to the water's edge, others with carefully preserved bushland, while still more had massive steep sides of sandstone, with houses perched on top.

Angus stood beside her at the rail, one arm round her waist, pointing out a tree, a bird, a tiny sailing skiff, his body talking to hers in a way that added magic to the boat trip.

The tall Norfolk pine trees along the beachfront at Manly reminded her of all the pictures she'd ever seen of Manly beach—so familiar it was hard to believe she was here. Or that she'd lived in Bondi for two years and had never been to Manly. Her life really had become restricted.

She hooked her hand through the arm of the man who'd brought her back to life, squeezing his arm in a silent thank you because words would never be enough to explain how wonderful she felt.

It was an idyllic day—the sun warm, with sufficient breeze to whip up a few foaming white horses on the ocean. Hand in hand, they walked the beach, then ate hot dogs at one of the tables on the esplanade.

The problem was it felt so right, being with

Angus, talking or not talking, holding hands, bodies close, doing their own communication. It felt like for ever, and she mustn't fall into the trap of thinking that way—mustn't be misled into imagining this was anything but here and now.

They made the most of the day, catching the fast ferry back to the Quay and a little one across to Luna Park, Angus having expressed disbelief that she'd never been there.

'Scared of heights?" he asked.

'Like I could rappel down to an injured victim on a cliff face if I was?' she teased.

'You do that?' he asked, so astonished she had to laugh.

'Mostly in training but once here and several times when I was in the SDR in Brisbane. We've mountains just north of the city—the Glasshouse Mountains—that idiots with no experience insist on climbing by the hardest route.'

He was leading her towards a Ferris wheel, and looking up to see the height of it she was very glad she wasn't afraid of heights. Although...

'You know, sitting in one of these swaying

cradles right at the top isn't quite the same as working on cliffs with a safety harness on and ropes attached to solid objects and team members around to make sure you're safe.'

He put his arm around her, pulling her closer.

'I'll anchor you,' he whispered, and for one wild moment it sounded like a promise of forever.

They rode up into the sky with stupendous views over the harbour and the city, then wandered through the park, eating fairy floss and hot dogs because that's what you ate at fairs. They rode the big dipper, Kate shrieking as they zoomed down the steep slopes, and got lost in the mirror maze.

To Kate, it was a magical experience—nothing more than going out and having fun really—but to somewhere new, and especially with someone, well, special, her whole being seemed filled with joy and happiness.

'And just what are you contemplating so seriously?' Angus asked, as they paused under a shady umbrella, eating ice cream.

She smiled at him but hesitated about answering. To be contemplating fun?

He'd think she was crazy!

Except she had been!

Having fun, that was.

Probably best not to mention the joy and happiness…

CHAPTER FIVE

IT HAD BEEN enough of a day to justify room service back at the hotel, and as Angus fed her fresh fruit and her body shivered in delight and anticipation, she found it hard to remind herself that it was just for now.

And later, much later, as they lay, still breathless, on the bed, with Angus nuzzling the sensitive spot behind her ear and whispering that he'd have to order room service more often, the thought of it not being just for now lodged in her head, and she put her arms around him and drew him close.

To hold him forever?

No, it couldn't be but for now they were together and if what she was beginning to feel felt like for ever, that was just too bad.

'Today we do the city!' Angus announced when they finally surfaced at close to ten in the morning. He added quote marks with his fingers, and although deep down he was thinking he'd just as soon spend the day in bed with Kate, something told him that would be a bad idea.

Being together twenty-four hours a day, doing simple things like sightseeing and fun park rides seemed to have shifted something inside him.

He couldn't define it and definitely didn't want to think about it too much, but it had somehow changed from a good idea to show someone around his city, to finding huge pleasure in that someone's company, and an awareness that this had become a very special time.

For Kate too, he was sure. To him, she seemed to grow more beautiful every day as if happiness was radiating from inside her.

While in bed—well, he wouldn't think about bed or they'd never leave the room. But her body seemed to match his in its ardour and excitement, in the intensity of some of their encounters and the soft, slow lovemaking of the early morning.

He knew he had to walk away from her—his life too uncertain, too chaotic for him to offer much in the way of a husband.

Husband!

Where the hell had that come from?

'Well, I'm done in the bathroom,' the subject of his concerns said, appearing in a pair of long tailored shorts, a blue patterned top, and a silly hat with orange sunglasses at the front perched on her head. He'd bought it for her at Luna Park the previous day, more as a joke than anything else.

'Urchin!' he said, and she laughed.

'I thought you'd like the hat,' she told him. 'It kind of finishes off the outfit.'

And as she stood there, clean and ready for the day, grinning at him from under the hat, he wanted nothing more than to get up off the bed, take her in his arms and hold her.

Possibly forever.

He pushed off the bed and dodged past her into the bathroom, dodging past just in case his arms reached out—

Perhaps, he thought when he was under the shower, not quite cold but cool enough, it was just because they were with each other all the time and having fun together—that would explain things.

Practical as that explanation was, it didn't sit

easily with him, so he set the matter aside and concentrated on their itinerary for the day.

Art gallery first, he decided, then...

They were halfway across the beautiful park leading eventually to the gallery when he stopped.

Kate had moved on another step but was pulled back by their joined hands.

'You do like art galleries, do you? I didn't ask. I love this one, and there's a super exhibition on at the moment.'

She smiled, came close, and kissed him lightly on the lips.

'I love them, big ones and little ones. They are the parts of Sydney I do know.'

An hour later, they were in a new exhibition of Australian aboriginal art when he felt his phone buzzing in his pocket.

Cursing inwardly, he pulled it out, praying it was something simple, an enquiry about the tent maybe—

'I've got to go!' he said, staring blankly at the message telling him to report to base ASAP and well aware his words were equally disbelieving. 'I'm so sorry, Kate. I was going to take you to the Queen Victoria Building after this, you can still go, and you can stay on at the hotel and have room service. I'll sort the bill when I pick up my car but I—'

She put her finger to his lips.

'You have to go,' she said. 'I do understand. I always understood it was just for now, and now has been tremendous fun. I'll stay on here at the gallery for a while and go to the arcade but probably go home to Alice tonight.'

He wanted to argue, but what about? This was his life.

He pulled her tight and kissed her hard, oblivious of the people around them.

Opened his mouth to say he would be in touch, then closed it again because would he?

Where was he being sent?

How long would he be away?

Would he even return?

He squeezed her hand and walked away, determined not to look back, not to check if she was as upset as he was, crying perhaps—not that he was crying.

Not on the outside anyway, and definitely not when walking through a public gallery, but he felt as if something had been wrenched out of his insides, out of his gut perhaps—couldn't be his heart...

He was halfway out the door, still battling to find a way through all the swirling emotion in his head—well, his head *and* his body—when he noticed the gift shop. Art gallery gift shops sold mostly books on art and classy posters, but they also sold top-of-the-range souvenirs.

Jewellery?

He ducked inside and was rewarded with an array of Australian gemstones set in earrings, bracelets, necklaces and—yes, just over there—a pendant.

It was an opal, radiating brilliant red and blue and green with flashes of gold as the sun caught it. To him, it seemed to exemplify all the colours of the happiness he and Kate had shared. He bought it, wrote a quick note on a card, and left it at the hotel when he went back there to get his stuff. She'd have to return there to pack and he wanted her to have it as she left the city—have something to remember him by, something as beautiful as their time together had been.

Now he could go back to work...

* * *

Kate watched him leave, waiting for him to turn, to wave, determined not to cry in case he did turn, wanting to cry when he didn't. Then, aware of the covert glances of the few people who'd been in this part of the gallery, she continued her inspection of the paintings, a little blurry perhaps, because she knew that 'now' was over.

From there she went to the Queen Victoria Building, the beautifully restored old building that housed some of the city's most expensive jewellery stores and small boutiques.

There, tucked into a corner on the upper level, she spotted a beautiful sign, scrolled in gold, Lady Marmalade! Intrigued, she went closer, and smiled as she saw the red velvet-covered antique chair in the window, a mannequin sitting demurely on it in black lace underwear.

With the taste of Angus still on her lips after their farewell kiss, she slipped inside. The exquisiteness of the garments stole her breath, and her fingers trembled as she touched sheer silk and delicate lace. She might never see Angus again, but the last few days had changed her in ways she barely understood.

Outwardly she might look the same, and she'd return to work as dedicated as ever, but inwardly she'd been awakened to such joy and happiness that it seemed only right she should celebrate it. *And*, she decided as she slid a few more hangers off the rails, having sexy underwear under her work clothes was as good a way as any. The slither of silk against her skin would keep her memories alive.

Keep her alive?

She returned to the hotel, considerably less well-off but with the pain of loss lessened just a little by her mad, impulsive buys. As she walked through the lobby, a receptionist called to her, handing her a package.

'Your friend left this,' she said, and, although intrigued, Kate slipped it into one of the carrier bags and went up to their room before she opened it.

Inside the package was a small white box, tied with blue ribbon, and inside that—

Her legs went from under her and she dropped down onto the bed, holding the opened box in both hands, staring in wonderment at the beautiful gem inside it.

'So you'll always remember our "now",' the note said. As if she'd ever forget it!

And as she sat there, on the bed, her fingers running lightly over the words Angus had written, she felt again the terrible pain that loss could bring—the ache inside her threatening to spoil her memories of the joy, and loving, and laughter.

Had Angus guessed this was how she'd feel that he'd sent this beautiful gift?

She picked it up, clenched it in her hand and sent a promise through the ether to wherever he was that she *would* remember.

She slipped it around her neck, fastened the catch at the back and smiled at her reflection.

How could she not?

Once packed, she had the concierge call a taxi for her and headed back home—to Alice and to real life, but to a better real life, she told herself. She owed it to Angus to get back to the Kate she had once been. He'd shown her the life she'd forgotten; the way life should be lived.

Oh, she'd still work as hard, and train for the SDR, but she'd start saying yes when the team went for a drink after training, and she'd take Alice out to dinner once a week.

As the taxi pulled up outside the apartment block and she found money to pay the driver, she wondered just how long these great resolutions would last.

And, more importantly, just how would they help heal the ache she felt inside, fill the emptiness in her heart?

Those questions were answered, or at least set aside, when she returned to work, where one of their almost cyclical busy weeks had already begun. Hurrying from theatre to theatre, being seconded to orthopods and gynaes, as well as working with her supervisor, Kate had no time to brood over Angus's departure, although she did try to call in and see Harriet at least once a week, bringing her news and gossip from the hospital and encouraging her to join her occasionally for a quiet dinner uptown.

Harriet's ex-boyfriend Pete had finally manned up enough to admit the relationship was over and had taken his toothbrush and shaver and what clothes he hadn't managed to sneak out during his 'disappearing' weeks.

Kate felt Harriet was taking it well, but when her new friend said rather bitterly, 'I no longer suited his image of us as the perfect couple,' Kate knew just how upset, how hurt Harriet had been by his defection.

Although a rather complicated camera sitting on the coffee table in Harriet's room did please Kate, as did Harriet's enthusiasm for her new hobby.

'I know you're right and I could spend all my time just taking photos from my balcony of all the different moods of the sea, but it's been great for my leg as it's got me out walking and I'm going a little further each day.'

'Good for you!' she told Harriet, before heading back to Alice's apartment to see what was for dinner.

So far her 'going out for a drink with the team' hadn't happened, but she and Harriet had become closer and one day, hopefully, she'd get off work early enough to actually go out—with anyone or no one, even for a walk on the beach.

Work did ease off and if the SDR team teased her a little when she joined them for a pizza after a meeting, she just smiled and laughed with them and actually felt enjoyment in the company.

She told herself she owed it to Angus to get

out more but the real upside was that working hard, chatting to Harriet or eating pizza with the team took her mind off the hollowness inside her, even if it was only temporarily.

At times, it seemed as if it was the physical side she missed so much—his closeness in the bed, the touch of his hand as they walked together, the way he slung an arm around her shoulders…

But she missed their talk as well, from work discussions, to what wine to drink with crab, to silly things about their youth. She'd been totally consumed by the man, and although she'd been left bereft, she worked on, and socialised, and tried desperately to fill this new emptiness inside her with whatever she could find.

Angus had been called not to a military or humanitarian disaster but to the far side of the country where the second of his prototypes was being manufactured. He'd incorporated various modifications into it, and the manufacturer had other projects lined up but was having difficulty with the new tent, hence the urgent summons.

So, although he spent what seemed like

twenty hours a day either arguing with the project manager at the factory, or writing up changes to the specifications into the wee hours of the morning, he found himself missing Kate.

And although he wasn't in any danger—except perhaps from increasing frustration—he reminded himself that his sudden departure from Sydney had been because of his job—a job that could just as likely taken him into a war zone.

But Kate had sneaked beneath his skin. He could feel her there, feel the way she moved against him, smell the scent of her shampoo on the pillow next to him, hear her chuckle at a silly joke—this last one when he was arguing with an increasingly bad-tempered project manager.

Highly inappropriate that he had smiled at the memory...

But this particular prototype had to be just right for it was going to a big convention in the US and the army was hoping for enough orders to balance out the considerable amount of money they had already spent on it, perhaps even enough to enable them to expand the programme.

So he worked and tried hard not to think about Kate, glad in some ways for the difficulties he was encountering so he had little time to brood over their short time together.

He'd done the right thing, he knew he had, in making it 'just for now', but now could have lasted a little longer, surely.

He could contact her when he got back to Sydney, hook up again—

And when the next call came?

Probably from China where components of the tents would be manufactured once they had the prototypes right, or would the army decide he'd been dithering around with this business for long enough and send him back into mainstream army life—Special Ops awaiting him if he wanted it.

Maybe the spirit-breaking training he'd have to do would take his mind off Kate!

The next call, when it came, was a relief from the seemingly endless petty problems that had had him tied in knots. Landslide in the Snowy

Mountains, several chalets affected, people trapped inside, and while he felt for all those injured or in danger, he also felt a thrill that his tent—had they brainwashed him at Bondi Bayside that he kept thinking of it that way—would finally be tested.

He figured, as he flew back to his base in an air force jet, that the mountains were probably closer to Melbourne, so disaster relief response would come from there.

He was being fed more information as they travelled. It was cold in the mountains, still too early for too much snow, although the snow blowers had been working on the slopes. Apparently, plenty of visitors had been taking advantage of the last of the cheaper off-season accommodation, so the affected lodges had been full.

Then there'd been rain in weather not quite cold enough to turn it into snow, and more rain, and more rain, and the sodden ground had shifted, just slightly at first but eventually carrying the ski lodges and the people inside them down into the river valley.

Floodwaters?

There'd be army engineers there by the time he arrived so that wouldn't be his problem.

Back at the base, helicoptered from the air force runway, he had a quick word to the commander, grabbed some clean clothes and a heavy, waterproof jacket, shoved the small pile of mail that had been just inside his door into one pocket, and headed back to where another helicopter waited, his precious tent and two add-on accommodation tents already packed inside, along with his regular support crew.

The view as they circled the mountains prior to landing was spectacular, but his attention was more on where they could set up their rescue mission. There was a relatively flat area below where the chalets had been, close to where they'd ended up, and he could see one helicopter already there.

'Enough room to land beside it?" he asked the pilot, and received a thumbs-up in reply.

The whine of the engines changed as the pilot decreased speed and within minutes they were on the ground, the crew already out, dragging the cumbersome bundles with them and carrying them to a clearing closer to the devastated buildings, unzipping and unfolding as they moved, working like a well-oiled machine.

Angus joined them and the chopper lifted away. He'd already seen the familiar SDR logo on the other helicopter, although it was probably a Victorian response unit.

Kate was crawling through a space the USAR team had shored up when she heard the helicopter.

Good, more help on the way!

She could hear the tap, tap, tap of wood on wood, the sound that had told the USAR team there was someone alive ahead of her. But although she called to the tapper, she received no reply, so it was only when she glimpsed the shoulder she alerted those up top to her find.

Because whoever it was couldn't speak? Crushed chest? The taps told her she was getting closer, although there were fewer of them and they were getting weaker.

Don't go beyond the red ribbon, the USAR fellow had said, but she could see the shoulder of someone just beyond it and there was no way she could stop now.

Very cautiously—she'd done an Urban Search

and Rescue training course herself—she moved what looked like a corner of a pool table, edging it sideways so she could see further into the wreckage.

It was a woman, blood colouring her blonde hair a deep pink.

'I'm here, we'll get you out,' she told the woman, although that could well prove to be a lie. More of the pool table—thankfully not slate—had fallen on the woman's legs and one leg of the table, thick, heavy wood, lay across her chest.

There was no room for her to get past the woman to try to lift the obstacles, so she dug, slowly and carefully, one small piece of rubble at a time. She could see the table leg was jammed at both ends so it wouldn't—shouldn't—give way as she excavated.

When she felt she had sufficient space cleared beneath the woman, she slid her arms beneath her shoulders and pulled as gently as she could.

A little movement!

She tried again. The table leg stayed stable as she edged the woman from under it, but the material that had come down on her legs was coming with them.

Talking all the time, she eased the woman inches closer, until she was free enough for Kate to examine her—well, the top half!

She pulled a thick triangular bandage from the bag that she had dragged along beside her, and found a decent-sized piece of timber to wrap it around it to support the woman's head.

Felt for a carotid pulse—regular, but weak—let her fingers feel around the scalp, an open wound but no ominous grating of bone or bone indentations to hint at skull fractures with likely brain damage.

If she could find the woman's hands, she could find a viable vein and start a drip, adding a little pain relief to keep the woman comfortable until someone could get to her. It was pointless calling for more help yet, as any helper coming in would have to use the same tunnel so would have to wait until Kate crawled out.

Hands were at the end of arms, so should be easy to find, but the first arm she felt carefully along had a piece of what felt like metal protruding from it. Heart hammering, Kate's fingers continued the exploration.

Not good! The metal—a rod as thick as her thumb—was through and through, the woman was held by whatever the rod was connected to. At least while it remained in place there'd be less bleeding, but remembering she'd already shifted the woman, Kate felt carefully around the entry and exit wounds and sighed with relief when she could find no extreme blood loss.

Best she get herself out and leave it to the experts. She'd give the woman pain relief and go for help.

Easier said than done. No room for turning so she had to inch backwards on her stomach, all the while being careful not to bump against any shoring props or anything else that might bring the whole building crashing down on her.

And her patient!

When it seemed as if she'd been worming backwards for ever, she felt someone take a good grip on her ankles and haul her the rest of the way out.

Paul!

He put out a hand to help her to her feet.

'I hope you didn't go further than the red ribbon,' he said with mock severity as she brushed dust and mud and sawdust from her clothes.

'Not much further but there's a badly injured

woman in there and we need to get her help *now*!'

'I'll get some of the USAR team back here,' he said, and jogged away, while Kate wiped more dust from her eyes and finally looked around.

Looked around in disbelief!

While she'd been deep in the bowels of the destroyed building, a huge white tent had appeared. A huge white tent with a red cross on the roof and a tall, broad-shouldered, angry-looking man bustling around it, yelling orders to the crew securing guy ropes and generally getting things shipshape.

Or tent-shape in this instance.

The crew were obviously not doing it quickly enough for Angus, who was acting as if imminent disaster might befall them all if his tent wasn't ready in whatever time-frame he'd promised. Of course he'd be anxious—this was the first trial of his tent in a real emergency situation, rather than the practice sessions it would have been through.

But although her feet wanted to cross the uneven ground towards him, and she could almost feel his presence on her skin, duty took her back to Blake, where she reported on the state of the woman and asked for her next job.

'In the tent if ever Angus gets it up to his satisfaction,' Blake said, finding a smile in spite of the chaos all around them. 'We've moved about four survivors into it already and Sam's in there with a couple of paramedics.'

So she'd get to be closer to Angus anyway, Kate thought, but after the initial flutter of excitement she'd felt at seeing him, she was now uneasy. The 'now' was over so how would he be? How should *she* be?

Casual, old friends—that would be the best way to play it, and forget excited nerve endings and little tugs low in her belly.

She headed for the tent.

CHAPTER SIX

As it happened, it wasn't until the end of a very long day spent dealing with casualties inside the tent that Kate caught up with Angus, who'd spent his entire day ironing out glitches in the setting up of the primary tent then erecting accommodation tents, army issue, for the relief workers, and a mess tent to feed the masses.

He came into the mess as she was in line to grab a hamburger, Paul behind her, telling how they'd managed to extricate the woman by opening another tunnel and coming in at a right angle to where she was trapped. She was one of the rescued who was airlifted to hospital without stabilisation in the tent, her injuries serious enough that another of the specialist doctors would stabilise her the best he could in flight.

Kate shook her head as she thought about the woman, knowing that the piece of steel would still be through her arm, no one wanting to move it in case it caused catastrophic bleeding.

'They had to put fire-retardant padding around her body because they needed a small, battery-operated angle grinder to cut through the steel to release her and it could have spat sparks.'

'The poor woman,' Kate was saying, when the hairs on the back of her neck stood to attention only a second before a deep voice said, 'Fancy meeting you here.'

Paul turned first, greeting Angus like an old friend.

'Look, Kate, it's Angus. I thought that tent was pretty special, and I wondered if it was his.'

Kate closed her eyes briefly. The way Paul spoke it was obvious the hospital gossip mill hadn't linked her and Angus.

She said thank you to the young soldier passing the hamburger and turned towards the man she'd thought she'd never see again. Not that seeing him again meant anything. She knew that! Knew the 'now' was over.

'Hi!' she said, as brightly as she could, considering that actually looking at him had sent her heart rate rocketing and she could feel blood drumming in her ears.

'Hi, yourself,' he said, his eyes moving over her as if to take in all of her, caressing her somehow.

Or perhaps it was just the smell of the hamburger making her feel weird.

'Your tent's fantastic to work in,' she told him, desperate to break what was becoming an awkward silence. Desperate to think of anything apart from touching him, feeling his skin beneath her hand, her body pressed to his...

But now Paul had been served they could both walk away.

'Just fantastic,' she added to Angus, and followed Paul to a table at the far side of the mess, hoping it looked as if she was walking normally, not fleeing from the man who, by simply being there, had thrown her body into turmoil.

Well, that went well, Angus thought to himself as she walked away. He turned to watch her until he realised he was probably drawing attention to himself, propped like a post in the middle of the mess.

And wasn't it for the best?

Didn't her brush-off—what else could you

call it?—indicate that she'd realised the time they'd had together was over?

Which it was, wasn't it?

Hadn't he set up the programme that way?

Explaining that because he never knew where he'd be from one day to the next, he couldn't offer permanence?

Except seeing her at a distance when someone had pulled her feet first out of a tunnel—dusty and dishevelled—his body had tightened and a strange pain in his chest had made breathing difficult for a moment.

And he'd certainly thought, once assured she was on her feet and okay, Great, we can get together again!

But that's what he'd done to Michelle—on and off—and not only had it not worked but it had hurt her, making her feel she was little more than a casual companion. Made her feel used, she'd once told him. Convenient.

He couldn't do that to Kate.

Because Kate was different?

Because he'd wanted to find out what had changed her, and he'd been pleased to see glimpses of the old Kate re-emerging as they'd enjoyed time together?

Hmm! He was thinking of excuses now—excuses so he could make the most of this unexpected reunion.

Hardly fair on Kate, though, would it be?

He walked out of the tent, dinner-less, too confused to stay inside, too aware with every fibre of his body of the woman sitting not twenty feet away from him.

Kate watched him go. Her outward reaction to seeing him must have been the right one—cool and casual so he would know she wasn't expecting their...whatever it had been would continue.

So why was there an ache right through her body and a heavy sadness pressing down on her chest?

Why was her inner reaction so...?

Wrong?

Paul was telling her about another rescue, and about a new lot of shoring the USAR team was putting through to the second building. There'd be work to do and if there was one thing she'd learned over the past few years, it was that work was the perfect way to blot everything else from her mind.

She finished her food and while Paul lined up for more, she went back outside to where the sunset was painting the snow on the higher mountains a rosy gold.

'There's a safe passage through to the other building now,' the site manager told her, repeating Paul's news, but this man pointed the way. 'As far as we know, there are at least three families in that lodge, not sure how many kids.'

Kate slung her bag over her shoulder, checked her pockets for gloves, and headed for the new tunnel.

Blake was at the end of it, supervising the removal of a man on a stretcher, easing the rigid equipment around a bend.

'Just do what you can,' he said. 'They've set up lights but it's still gloomy in places. Check under anything that might have been a bed or a table for kids that were pushed there to shelter.'

Kate nodded, going forward now the stretcher had passed, joining other relief workers on what was, for now, the front line.

A quiet sobbing took her to the right, stepping carefully over broken timber and shattered windows, glad her boots and tough overalls were at least protecting her body. The noise was coming from down near her feet, so she knelt, very tentatively, making sure the ground was solid beneath her knees in case she sent debris raining down on someone.

'Hello. Can you hear me?'

Wait ten seconds and call again, but before she got to ten, a little voice said, 'Here.'

Great! Kate thought, but at least the child— the voice had been a child's—could speak.

It had come from a mess of bedding and broken wood, and Kate poked her arm in underneath as far as she could.

'Can you see my arm?' she asked, waving her hand about as much as she dared.

A tight grip on one finger gave her the answer, and she pulled out her torch and bent lower so she could see beneath the mass of damage.

'I'm going to shine a torch so shut your eyes for a minute,' she said, keeping hold of the little hand that had now sneaked into hers.

Lying flat again, she shone the torch and made out the face of a small girl, eyes shut tight.

Shining it away from her face but deeper into the hole where the girl was, she said, 'You can open them now and have a look around. Can you move your legs and arms—just a little bit?'

'Yes,' came the answer. 'I was in another place and I couldn't find Mummy and so I crawled in here.'

'Good girl,' Kate said, bringing the torch back to shine on her own face. 'I'm Kate. What's your name?'

'Libby.'

'Okay, Libby, I need the torch to look around to see how we can make a hole big enough for you to get through, then if I need some help to make it safe for you, I'll give you the torch so you can hold it while you wait for me to get back. Okay?'

The answering 'Okay' was so wavery and soft that Kate looked desperately around the tangled material to see if she could get Libby out without calling in someone to shore up a hole.

The damaged mattress she could see was good. It was slung between two what must have been wall joists and would form a stable roof. If she could get Libby that far she'd be safe while Kate shifted other obstacles.

'Need help?'

It *would* be Angus and, for all she knew she wouldn't, she could have hugged him. Although with both of them now stretched prone on the ground that was hardly possible anyway.

'Little girl, Libby, just through there,' she said, ignoring the totally inappropriate reactions of her body to Angus's presence by her side. 'Libby, here's Angus and he's going to help us. He's big, and brave, and strong, so we'll soon get you out.'

'My daddy's big and brave and strong,' Libby told him and Kate found herself smothering a smile.

Angus had shifted, getting carefully to his knees so he could see over the trap in which the little girl was caught.

'I think there's a sturdy piece of timber over there that I can get without bringing anything down on top of us.'

'That would be nice, then what do we do?' Kate asked, totally focussed now on the child they had to rescue.

'I poke it in very carefully until it's beside Libby then I can use it as a lever to cautiously raise the mess in front of her and she should be able to scramble forward—'

'To under the mattress!' Kate finished for him. 'I'd worked out that bit just not how to get her that far.'

She looked at the piece of timber Angus was now holding, and pictured how far in it would have to go to work as a lever.

'I'll wiggle in a little further,' she said, 'so I can guide it past where Libby is then ease her out.'

'You stay right where you are,' Angus told her.

This time she chuckled. She knew it was probably adrenalin making her a bit silly, but to have Angus squatting there bossing her about—well, it was just too bizarre.

And as she was already wiggling forward, what was he going to do about it?

She found the end of the timber he was using and guided it, talking all the while to Libby, explaining, checking she was okay.

Though what was 'okay' in this situation?

Once they had the timber in place, Angus lifted it cautiously, and Kate was able to grasp both of Libby's hands and pull her gently with her as she, Kate, wiggled backwards.

The timber had lifted whatever had been

blocking Libby's passage closer to Kate as well, so she could pull the child right through.

'There was absolutely no need for you to go that far in,' Angus was saying crossly when she was finally able to sit up and lift Libby onto her knees.

Kate looked up at him and smiled, then began to examine the little girl for any injuries, Angus crouching beside them now, his arm around them both, making it difficult for Kate to concentrate on what had to be done.

Libby was scratched and bruised in places, but shock was the most likely thing to be affecting her right now so, easing away from Angus, Kate just sat and held her, rocking her back and forth, feeling the little arms clasped around her neck and praying that Mummy and big, brave, strong daddy were still alive somewhere.

Angus watched them, sensing the child needed the reassurance of Kate's arms around her, and Kate's soft words of comfort, but something in the way Kate had bonded with the child, the way she held her so tightly—a precious bundle in her arms—bothered him slightly. As if there was something deeper going on.

Unless what was bothering him was the image of a woman and child—like a mother and child—like a family…

Or that he'd had to watch as she'd put herself in danger to get to the child.

He shook his head, trying to clear the—was it frustration? Or simply the situation itself, being with Kate yet not with her, being distracted by her presence when all his attention should be on the job at hand?

'Okay,' she finally said. 'I think I'll pass you up to Angus and he can take you out to see the helicopters and the tents and all the stuff we've got out there to rescue people like you.'

Realising it was his cue, he turned to lift the little girl and caught the glint of tears on Kate's cheeks.

He moved away, bent double for the first few yards. He had to go. There was work to be done, but not stopping to comfort Kate—or to puzzle out what had brought on those shining tears—was one of the hardest things he'd ever done.

* * *

Kate was emerging from the tunnel a little later when a dishevelled and slightly bloody woman caught her arm.

'I heard there was a child rescued,' she said, panic making her voice rise with each word.

'What's your child's name?' Kate asked her, holding the woman's arm to steady her.

'It's Libby, Libby, and she's only six.'

Kate gave the woman a quick hug.

'And she's brave as a barrow full of bears,' she told the mother. 'You'll find her in the white tent, probably with a tall guy in army fatigues.'

The woman took flight, her feet barely touching the ground beneath her, obviously not feeling the cold or anything other than relief.

Kate watched her go, praying that big, brave, strong Daddy had also been found and at least one family could be reunited. She headed back down the tunnel. The USAR team, or maybe the army equivalent of it, had made branch tunnels off the main one and every one of them would have to be investigated. The USAR would have gone through their search routine, calling out to survivors, and Kate imagined that, by now, most of the victims they found would be unconscious.

As the new tunnel diminished in height, she bent, and then crawled her way along it. There'd been two families in this building—where was the other one?

Paul had found a man, wedged in a space beneath a fallen refrigerator, and a quick glance told Kate why they wouldn't be moving it in a hurry as it was holding up a tangle of shattered building material that might once have been kitchen cupboards.

'He said his foot was bleeding before he passed out, possibly from pain, and I've managed to get a faint pulse in his neck but if he's losing blood fast—'

'We need pressure bandages and a tourniquet,' Kate finished for him.

She was studying the space beside the man. Paul had been able to get close enough to feel for the carotid, for a pulse, but she was reasonably sure she could slide down beside him. Though whether far enough for her to check his foot, she wasn't sure.

'I'll try to get in there,' she said to Paul, and the team had been together long enough to know that sometimes only a woman *could* reach into certain places, and he didn't argue.

Angus would!

The thought, coming out of the blue when she'd been totally focussed on the problem in front of her, sent a jolt of annoyance through her body.

And a bit of warmth as well, she had to admit. It was nice to have someone thinking of her safety for all they should both be concentrating one hundred per cent of their intention on their jobs.

She eased under the refrigerator, pausing to check there was still a pulse in the man's neck, counting his breaths—slow and steady. As the space narrowed she was forced to turn onto her side and crab along like that, as close to the man's body as a lover.

And she knew why that description had come to mind—Angus again.

Focus!

Whatever had happened between her and Angus was in the past, and that's where it would stay. She'd reached the man's thighs and felt carefully around the one closest to her, shoving her hand to get it underneath, feeling for obstructions.

But that one, at least, was free, although the other was under a tangle of crockery and she didn't have time to waste clearing it.

Just a little further, not far now, edging past knees and on down to his feet.

Or what was left of his feet.

One seemed to be intact but the other had been partially severed, possibly by a sheet of glass, right across beneath the toes. A complete amputation might have caused the blood vessels to shrink back and close defensively, but this was bleeding profusely.

Hauling her bag up towards her, she took out gauze padding and clamped it on the injury, holding it tightly with her hand, applying all the pressure she could, packing more gauze against it when it was still bleeding after what had seemed like an hour but was only ten minutes.

'Have a man in blue tunnel,' she said into the mouthpiece on her helmet, glad she'd noticed the colour of the ribbons on this one. 'Bleeding profusely from a partial amputation of his left foot. He must be trapped by his other leg as we can't move him. The injured leg is free.'

She added more gauze then bandaged the wound as tightly as she could, lying on her side in a space more suited to a rabbit.

Tourniquet?

She had a commercially produced one in her bag, but there were pros and cons.

She glanced back at the blood seeping now through the bandages, and reached for the tourniquet, slipping it out of its plastic bag and swiftly getting the strap in place around the man's lower leg, just above the ankle. She tightened the strap and buckled it then used the small rod to wind it even tighter—noted the time using a stylus on the small screen attached to her overalls above her top pocket. Waited for a minute, then removed the padding from the wounded foot. There was still blood seeping out but it would be controllable with the gauze and a new bandage.

Now she could feel around the other leg to see if she could find the obstruction that was holding him, praying that it would be something fixable and they wouldn't have to amputate the man's trapped leg in order to free him. He'd already lost half a foot.

'Hop out and let me see what I can do,' a male voice said.

The man was in USAR overalls, and although he was larger than Kate, she wasn't surprised to see him sit down beside the injured man and sinuously work his way in.

'Feet first so I can see what's above him,' he said to Kate. 'You said it's his right leg that's trapped?'

Kate agreed, while the newcomer felt all around the refrigerator, testing its stability.

'Seems solid,' he said. "I'm Charlie, by the way.'

'Kate.'

'Well, Kate, I don't think we can lift the fridge to get at him,' he said, and Kate refrained from telling him she'd already figured that out.

'The fridge is holding this partition down and it's the end of the partition or whatever it was that's landed on his leg.'

Kate had swabbed the man's hand and was inserting a cannula, preparing to start some fluid running into him, but she understood what Charlie was saying.

Not only understood, but also realised they were getting closer and closer to a nasty solution to the problem.

Satisfied she'd done what she could for the moment, she checked the fluid bag she'd left resting on the fridge and made sure the line was clear, then backed away until the tunnel was high enough for her to stand.

Not wanting the man's situation to be broadcast to everyone, she made her way to the tent in search of Blake. If the limb had to be amputated, they would have to prepare the necessary equipment.

'A team member from USAR will contact me if we need to go back in,' she told Blake, whose face already looked grey with fatigue.

'Well, you take a break,' he told her. 'Maybe in the mess. I'll call you if you're needed.'

Kate nodded. Her body told her it would rather rest on a bed, but Blake was right. If they had to amputate, he'd need her there.

CHAPTER SEVEN

SHE WAS LEAVING the tent when she realised that on shelves that had miraculously appeared along its side, and were apparently held up by air, were stacks of equipment. In fact, everything she needed to restock her bag.

She replaced all the items she'd used, ticking each one off a list on a clipboard on the shelves.

Slinging her bag back over her shoulder, she headed for the mess.

Angus had been treating a woman with crush injuries to her left arm and shoulder, splinting the arm to keep it stable as she was airlifted to hospital.

Had he sensed Kate's presence in the tent that he wasn't surprised when he looked up to see her speaking seriously to Blake?

The thought was disturbing. Hadn't he always prided himself on giving one hundred per cent of his attention to whatever he was doing?

He shook away the notion and concentrated on securing his patient to the stretcher.

But as Kate stopped near the entrance to replenish her supplies, he came abreast of her as his patient was wheeled out towards one of the helicopters, both now ferrying the injured and their families to hospitals.

'Are you taking a break?' he asked, when he'd said goodbye and good luck to his patient.

'Just until Blake needs me,' she said, explaining about the possible amputation.

'I could assist with that,' he said, thinking it might spare Kate the horrifying sight of a field amputation.

She looked up at him, a glint in her eyes.

'Think I can't take it?' she challenged, and he had to laugh.

Though when he spoke, he was serious—speaking softly, gently.

'I think you could take whatever life threw at you.'

The glance she shot him was startled, and he imagined she'd grown a little paler, but as she straightened her shoulders and colour returned to her cheeks, she said, 'I might take you up on that offer to assist Blake. I think a quick nap would do me more good than another meal or even a hot drink in the mess.'

'If that hamburger is all you've had to eat today, you need some real food. Come on, I'll pull rank and get you a decent meal then even find a bed for that nap.'

He went to sling his arm around her shoulders, but she moved away, whether deliberately or not he didn't know, although he was glad she did. Neither of them would enjoy being gossiped about if people thought they were interested in each other.

Because they weren't, were they?

Well, not now—not after the now...

Much as he wanted to, he could hardly bang his hand to his head either, but he needed to get it straightened out—concentrate on work, not emotion.

He scanned the blackboard menu as they entered the mess, and decided on the rich beef stew for himself, pleased when Kate agreed it would be just the thing for a cool night in the mountains.

Sending her to find a table, he got the meals himself, bringing them across to where she sat beside one of the 'windows' in the mess tent.

'The night is so light—bright with stars, I suppose,' she said, thanking him when he set down the meal but continuing to look out the window, colleagues, nothing more. 'We don't really see stars in the city.'

So they talked of stars, and the city, and he told her how overwhelmed he'd been by the stars in the Sahara—finding it hard to believe there could be so many of them when the night skies he was used to had so few.

'So few visible,' Kate reminded him, and he smiled at her.

'I sometimes wonder if a lot of things aren't visible in the city,' he said.

'Like homelessness,' she suggested. 'We get so used to seeing people sleeping in doorways we don't stop to think about what horror they've known in their lives to have ended up there.'

He shook his head, surprised yet not surprised at her reaction.

'Here I am thinking about emotions, how the everyday rush and hurry in the city, the need to earn enough to be able to live in the place, can overwhelm the things in which we should find joy, like looking at the stars or walking on the beach. And you come up with homelessness, which is, of course, only too true. We don't look hard enough'

She smiled at him, but he felt it was a polite smile, nothing more, no hint of the Kate who'd been coming to life only a few weeks ago— the one who would use her fingers to stifle a chuckle at something absurd.

'The man Blake's with is in the blue tunnel,' she reminded him, in case he hadn't got the message that they were here to work, not chat about stars and life in the city. Let alone emotions. 'And the bed?'

He stood up, collecting their plates so he could drop them over at the servery, and led the way out of the mess.

'It's just a basic tent, I'm afraid,' he said. 'Shared facilities and hot beds, with someone dropping into one the moment it's vacated.'

She half smiled.

'I didn't expect five stars,' she assured him.

They found an empty bed, complete with a sleeping bag opened up to act as a duvet.

'Pull it over you,' Angus said. 'You won't realise how cold it is until your body relaxes.'

He paused, sure there was more to say—more

he wanted to say—but only silence stretched between them.

Kate thanked him, and dropped her bag at the end of the bed before slumping down on it, suddenly so tired she knew she would sleep just as she was, not even bothering to remove her boots.

Not even sparing a thought for all her physical reactions generated by Angus's re-emergence in her life.

It was only temporary anyway, and the work was so important she could ignore them.

Most of the time...

She set the alarm on her watch to wake her in an hour, and lay down, only vaguely aware that Angus was still standing there.

'Blue tunnel,' she reminded him, before she closed her eyes and slept.

'Like intern year all over again,' she muttered to herself when the alarm hauled her back to consciousness. Back then, sometimes on duty far beyond the twelve rostered hours, grabbing an hour's sleep had been the only way to keep going, but she'd forgotten how fuzzy she'd always felt when she woke up.

Like now. Her head full of cotton wool.

A quick but surprisingly hot shower partly restored her, and a coffee and pastry in the mess completed the job. The army sure knew how to live!

A new site commander was organising things from above the ruins and he directed her back to where she'd first been.

'They've shored up a lot more of the wreckage in there,' he told her, 'and they're trying to get through to a small group of survivors—talking to them and all.'

So back down to the red tunnel, trying hard to think of the survivors they might rescue, rather than the man who'd virtually put her to bed an hour ago.

But how could she not think of him?

For weeks she'd been trying to shut away the memories of their time together, trying to box them up to look at far in the future when thinking about him wouldn't be so painful.

It shouldn't have been, she knew that.

It had been a brief affair, nothing more, but those magical days in Sydney, although cut short, had made her realise—

No, she wouldn't go there!

Couldn't go there!

Red tunnel, concentrate on that.

She found the team working to get to this group of survivors—five, they told her—in an offshoot of the tunnel she knew, and joined them in lifting rubble, piece by careful piece, aware from the sounds beyond them that the little group was doing the same thing on their side. And as they moved debris on their side, a couple of soldiers shored up the new length of tunnel, making sure the rescue workers stayed safe.

They were almost through when an ominous creaking above made everyone pause.

'Don't touch anything,' one of the army rescuers shouted through to the survivors, before radioing for an engineer to get down there fast.

They were all peering upward, trying to figure out what might be shifting above them, while the silence from the other side sent an uneasiness through the rescuers.

It was probably inevitable that Angus arrived with the engineer.

'You could have slept longer,' he said to Kate, who was so busy trying to cope with all her physical reactions to his presence—the ones that wouldn't go into that damn box—she just ignored him.

Until he moved closer, stood right behind her and touched her lightly on the shoulder.

'The engineer will be a while figuring out the best way forward,' he said. 'Why don't you take another rest? I'll stay in case they need a doctor.'

Kate turned to look at him, her fingers curling into balled fists so she didn't reach out to touch his cheek, his arm, any bit of him.

'You look worse than I do,' she told him. 'Why don't you take a break?'

'Who me? A soldier? Take a break?'

He tried to look shocked but all he looked was more tired, and Kate could feel her heart aching for him. Aching to help him, to look after him, to hold him and—

Yes, to love him!

She turned away, hoping he wouldn't see her thoughts written on her face or in her eyes.

Where had love come into it? she demanded of herself as she moved back a little way up the tunnel to let the team do their work.

And when?

Surely not right back at the island, for all

her heart had lurched at the sight of him in the SDR meeting.

Maybe as they'd sat together beside wee Joshua's grave—or perhaps on the Ferris wheel high above the harbour when the world had been a magical place, she and Angus the only inhabitants.

It must have sneaked in, a subconscious knowing, just waiting for a propitious moment to firm in her head.

Not that this was anything like a propitious moment! She was trying not to think about him at all, so definitely didn't want to consider what she felt might just possibly be love.

He was working beside the engineer, his broad back towards her, and though suitably and completely covered in army fatigues, she saw it as she had in bed, the flat planes of muscle around his shoulders, the shape of his vertebrae that she'd touched with fingertips—

And the thoughts she couldn't keep away when she was studying him sneaked back into her mind. The 'would the baby' thoughts—useless comparisons—the past she thought she'd conquered finding its way into the present—

Focus!

The rescuers were now passing rubble back along the tunnel, hand to hand, others now joining the line that stretched out into the open air.

Desperate to think about anything other than Angus's back, Kate squeezed into a space, passing debris with the best of them.

'You got gloves?' the woman beside her said quietly, and she stepped back for a minute to pull her heavy gloves from a pocket down the leg of her overalls and fit them on snugly.

It became mechanical—take a bundle from the woman on one side and pass it on to the man on the other, the movement gaining a rhythm of its own, so she was surprised when she looked up to see how much further they had gone, edging little by little towards the survivors.

'Are you free?'

Blake's voice in her helmet jolted her slightly, and once again she stepped out of the line, this time making her own way to the mouth of the tunnel, already telling Blake she was on her way.

Angus, answering a call on his headphones, followed her, realising she, too, must have been contacted for something more urgent than moving rubble.

As ever when he saw her, or was in her presence, his skin tightened with a sensory awareness that was hard to ignore, for all he knew he had to be totally focussed on the job.

Lives depended on it.

Blake Cooper was standing with the site manager and one of Angus's colleagues beside what looked like a newly opened tunnel.

Except when they got there, he hard on Kate's heels, it was more a steep shaft than a tunnel.

'From what we can make out, there's a badly injured woman down there.'

Silence greeted the remark, all of them only too aware they'd passed the thirty-hour mark since the buildings had collapsed, and the hope of finding anyone still alive was lessening by the minute.

'The USAR have done their best to make it safe but the space they've managed to shore up is too narrow for you or me to get in there, Angus.'

He turned to Kate.

'You've already done more than your share of crawling into tight spaces,' he said. 'Are you up for one more? Be honest about it. No one's going to think less of you if you say no. We don't want you going in only to find you're too exhausted to get out.'

'I can find a soldier to do it,' Angus said.

But Kate shook her head.

'If she's injured maybe there's something I can do, and if I can't make it out at least I can stay with her. I'm sure you lot would eventually dig down to us.'

She was looking at Angus as she spoke, making light of it, but his tight mouth and undoubtedly clenched teeth told her just how much he disapproved of the idea.

Someone had rigged up a rope and harness, insisting she should wear the harness even though the shaft sloped gradually at first.

'At least this way we can haul you out if we need to,' the USAR man told her.

She tightened the harness around her chest, checked that her bag was secure, and went cautiously into the sloping shaft. Easy going initially. She had to bend slightly but that was okay, then as the gradient grew steeper and the shaft walls began to close in on her, she sat and worked her way down on her backside, glad of the harness, even happier that whoever had tunnelled down here had been able to string some lights along one side.

She used her boots as brakes to slow her progress as the gradient grew steeper, not wanting to slide full tilt into the injured woman.

But now the shaft widened and levelled out slightly, and Kate realised it had been specifically dug to get to the lowest section of the ruined lodges.

Some parts were shored, but she guessed if the woman lay that way she'd have been found.

'Can you hear me?' she called, praying for an answer.

Nothing!

She shone her torch, deep into the wreckage.

'Can you hear me?'

This time a movement of some kind—over to the right—not distinct, more a slight shuffle.

The other rescuers had heard a woman!

She shone her torch to the right, asking this time, 'Can you see the light?'

The faintest of moans, but at least Kate now knew where to look.

She could see a space that seemed stable some way in. All she had to do was get there.

On hands and knees she started forward,

lying down to slither under beams, pushing herself forward with her feet, crawling where she could, talking all the time, telling whoever was there that she was coming.

The woman, when she finally came to her, was sheet white and barely conscious. A trail of blood going back into the rubble told Kate she'd already made her way through a lot of debris.

Now she lay on her back, blood seeping from her body, too far gone to answer even the simplest of questions.

With space to move, Kate set up fluids before beginning any examination of her injuries, instinct telling her there was something seriously wrong. But it took a long moan from the woman and a reflex writhing motion for Kate to realise the significance of the blood.

She ran her hands over the woman's abdomen, felt it tighten as she examined it, then relax, flaccid—empty!

And between the woman's legs, the placenta she'd just delivered, the cord that should have connected it to a baby now severed.

The baby! Where was the baby? She had to find the baby.

But the woman was bleeding more heavily

now, too much blood added to what she'd already lost.

Post-partum haemorrhage.

Kate pressed down hard on her patient's belly, hoping to seal off the offending blood vessel, but the blood kept coming.

And somewhere in the wreckage there was a baby—a newborn.

She breathed deeply, closing her eyes and willing herself back under control, thinking, thinking, thinking.

Then a remembered picture from some book she'd studied flashed into her mind. Lacking medical help, post-partum bleeding could be handled manually.

First, pressure on the abdomen, pressing downwards, holding it—hopeful the damaged vessel would close of its own accord.

No luck—the bleeding continued.

Back to the remembered picture.

Twisting her mike so she could speak into it, she knelt between the woman's legs and carefully inserted one gloved hand into her body, using her other hand on the woman's belly, pressing down against her own hand as hard as she could.

Now she could speak.

'I need a collapsible stretcher sent down on a rope. Woman with post-partum haemorrhage and no sign of the baby. Once I have her free of the debris and ready for you to lift, you'll have to pull me too because the only way I've been able to stem the bleeding is manually.'

Someone up there would get the picture, she told herself, and hopefully have blood products and anticoagulants on hand for the woman as soon as they reached the top.

There's a baby somewhere...

She had to fight the thought, fight even harder the urge to go and look.

Rattling noises, dirt coming down the shaft and Kate was glad she and her patient were clear of it.

But someone *had* understood—understood enough to send down a slightly built soldier with the stretcher.

'Reckoned you'd need help,' the new arrival—a young woman soldier—said, and Kate smiled with relief.

'Can you slide the stretcher through that opening?' she asked, shining her torch along the hole she'd crawled through.

'No worries,' said the cheerful woman, and she set to, threading the long, narrow, well-packed stretcher under and around obstacles until it reached Kate.

Who now had a dilemma.

No way could she keep up the pressure on the woman's uterus *and* load her on the stretcher.

She lifted her top hand and fished in her bag for a tightly folded cloth that could be fashioned into a sling, or if necessary used as a towel for messy hands.

Carefully she removed her other hand, wiped it swiftly on the bandage and began to unpack the stretcher, sliding one side in under the woman's body, then rolling her slightly to click the other side into place.

The bleeding continued, so as quickly as she could she wrapped the stretcher's wings around the woman's upper body and tightened straps to keep her securely in place. Pulled on a clean glove and once again invaded the poor woman's body to apply pressure on the bleeder.

'Now, if you can pull the stretcher towards you, I'll do what I can to push with my knees, but once we get her out to where you are, you'll have to go up the shaft to give the two of us room to be pulled up.'

'I could take over from you,' the soldier, now introducing herself as Laura, said.

And I could look for the baby.

The thought sneaked into Kate's mind but she pushed it away. What point in finding the baby if the mother died through blood loss that she, Kate, might be able to prevent.

Laura somehow got them back to the bottom of the shaft, then, aided by her harness and rope, made her way up to the top.

'Call when you're ready to come up,' a voice yelled from above.

'Anytime now,' Kate answered, 'but pull us slowly as we're coming up in tandem.'

And slowly but surely they made their way to the top, where waiting hands unhooked both the stretcher and Kate, and carried the patient, Kate still bent over her, still applying pressure, into the tent.

'We've got one of our gynaes up on the screen in a live feed from the hospital,' Blake told her as the woman, now free of Kate, was lifted onto an operating table. 'We'll take it from here.'

Kate nodded, anxious to get away and get

cleaned up—even more anxious to get back down that shaft.

Would they let her?

The thought made tears prick at the corners of her eyes.

Of course they would, she told herself as she stripped off and stepped under the shower.

Where tears really didn't matter as it was all water running down her cheeks.

She had no clean underwear or a clean overall, and she was running short of gloves, but she'd noticed piles of clothes just inside the door of the facilities tent.

Khaki but who cared! Wrapped in a towel, she already had underwear sorted—a singlet would do instead of a bra—and was checking out a thick sweater that would keep her warm under her overalls when Angus appeared.

'Stealing army clothes, are you?' he teased, and, startled, she turned towards him, not having felt his presence as she usually did.

'It's okay, that's what they're there for, but I wouldn't bother putting overalls back on, you need a proper break. A new response team has arrived, so it's time to sleep—perhaps eat something and then sleep.'

But Kate clutched the overalls to her, backing towards the privacy of the shower stall, so anxious to get back down that shaft and start looking for the baby she didn't stop to argue.

'Kate?'

He sounded puzzled—perhaps anxious.

'Not just now, Angus. I really do have to get back down there.'

She shut the screen between them and pulled on her purloined clothes—including the overalls and, oh, the bliss of clean socks!

Angus stared at the screen. Okay, she'd closed it in case someone else came in and saw him staring at her getting dressed, except it wasn't modesty or possible embarrassment at all, it was to shut him out—or maybe off! To stop him arguing with her, which he fully intended doing. She must be exhausted and he knew only too well that that's when accidents happened.

Yet when she reappeared, everything clean but her boots, it was to hurry past him, hurrying not to the tent to see how the woman she'd rescued was but back to the shaft, jogging now for all she'd said she didn't jog.

He wanted to follow her, to try to stop her, to

speak to whoever was in command over there and order she be stopped.

He gave a huff of despairing laughter.

Like she'd thank him for that!

He headed for the tent instead. Surely there he'd find a clue to her impetuous flight.

Blake's face was bleak, although the woman on the table in front of him looked relatively uninjured.

'She'll be okay,' Blake said. 'We've stopped the bleeding and they'll fly her straight out.'

'And the problem?'

Blake hesitated, shook his head and finally explained.

'She's just given birth,' he said quietly. 'There's a baby down there somewhere.'

A picture of Kate as she held the little girl, Libby, in her arms, flashed through Angus's head. Kate holding her tightly, tears on Kate's face...

A baby?

Had there been a baby somewhere in her life?

Or did she just long for one?

He knew she was estranged from her parents, who hadn't understood—or bothered to understand—why she'd cancelled her wedding.

Would a baby be someone for her to love—
someone to love her?

He had no idea but he did know, for certain,
that it was the baby that had taken her back
down that shaft.

He shook his head as he realised just how little he knew about the woman he loved.

Loved?

Hadn't he recoiled from that thought once
before?

But that must be it, love, and now she was
in danger.

Might be in danger.

Turmoil he'd rarely if ever felt was gripping
his body, while his thoughts ran riot in his head.

He left the tent, intending to go down to the
head of the shaft, but paused. He'd only be in
the way, and if Kate *was* down there he certainly didn't want to distract any of the people
up top who'd be responsible for her safety.

So?

First things first—start thinking clearly.

He'd eat and maybe rest—no, no way he
could rest.

He'd eat and…

His mind went blank again.

He needed a distraction—any distraction—something to focus on...

Mail, there was mail!

He clutched at the idea, something positive he could do. Anything to take his mind off Kate down some deep tunnel...

He'd eat then check that great wad of mail he'd picked up on his way through the base, whenever that had been. Probably mostly rubbish but maybe something from family—cousins who kept in touch in a spasmodic fashion, all posted on from base to base as he was transferred or out on missions.

And there was usually something from someone—in India, or Angola, anywhere, in fact—wanting details of the tent.

Tent!

Damn those Bondi Bayside people—he couldn't think of it by any other name, even to himself!

Kate inched her way forward, tugging at the rope she dragged behind her to keep it free from snags. The only way she'd been allowed back down the shaft had been by promising not to detach it, no matter how awkward it might become.

The passage through to where the woman had been was easier to negotiate now, much of the rubble knocked away as the stretcher had gone in and out. But once there, Kate knew she had to be careful. The trail of blood she'd seen when she'd first arrived suggested that the woman had crawled to the space in search of a way out or help of some kind. What Kate had to do was find that trail and follow it, being careful that she didn't obliterate it with a less than cautious step.

First she listened, listened for a cry. Surely a newborn would be crying?

Hypothermia. Even if the woman had managed to wrap the baby it would still be suffering from the cold, and in that case unable to cry.

Carefully threading her way through the crushed building, on hands and knees most of the time, slithering on her stomach at others, she followed the trail of blood.

It ended abruptly, and Kate peered around in the gloom, shining her torch into every crack and crevice, sure the baby must be here somewhere.

There *had* to be a baby!

Over there!

About three feet further in—

A bundle of what could be rags, motionless and silent.

Dead?

Kate refused to believe it. From somewhere a random bit of information flashed through her head—something about a newborn being able to live for up to three days untended.

But probably not in these cold conditions; probably not suffering from hypothermia. Although wasn't hypothermia good for injured people at times?

One part of her mind was thinking these things while the other part worked out how she could get to where the bundle was—so near and yet so far at the moment.

If she moved that blue board a bit to one side she could reach through…

First, see what else might move with the blue board. She didn't want to bring half a ski lodge down on the baby.

She moved the blue board, very slowly and cautiously, checking all the time whether anything else was moving with it.

So far, so good!

A little more and she could prop her end of it on that timber over there and—

Another ominous creak sounded above her and she stopped, but it was soon followed by a crash somewhere out of sight, so she knew she hadn't caused it.

She propped the blue board on the timber she'd chosen and reached through the gap she'd made to retrieve the bundle.

What if it wasn't the baby?

The thought made her pause, but only for an instant. She grabbed the bundle and lifted it, backing with it out to the relative safety of the space where the woman had been.

Now she could check it, see...

The baby was still, so still Kate feared the worst.

Lips tinged with blue.

She lifted it—him—and cleared his mouth, blew warm air into his mouth and nose. Then, with him still wrapped, she pressed her fingers to his carotid pulse. Nothing, then the faintest flicker. Keeping him wrapped as best she could, she used two fingers to compress his chest, counting as she went. The faint pulse was still there. She had to warm him. She tugged him out of the old black parka in which he had been wrapped and, ripping open her overalls, she hauled up her singlet and the sweater, and tucked the baby inside, against her skin, manoeuvring him up so his head was near the top and she could feel for breath and warm his lungs with her breath.

She put her hands on his back, warming him with her body heat, willing him to stay alive.

'You'll be okay,' she whispered against the little head. 'You'll be okay.'

Remembering tales of people suffering from hypothermia getting up off tables in the morgue—definitely exaggerated as most morgue stories were.

But hypothermia shut the body down to maybe one breath a minute and a negligible pulse.

'All okay?'

The voice in her ear startled her. She'd been supposed to keep talking to the people up the top, or at least make positive noises occasionally.

'All okay,' she said, although she wasn't at all sure it was.

But she held the baby close and breathed warm air into him until she knew she had to move—knew more and better help awaited this child up at the top.

'So let's get up there,' she whispered to him, and she began to worm her way back to the bottom of the shaft, where she signalled she was ready to be hauled up.

The crowd at the top startled her even before the great roar went up. Charlie had come over to help her out of the harness, now fitted only around her waist.

'Someone heard you talking to the baby and the word spread like wildfire. I think everyone needed a good news story as they've found a few more bodies.'

'But I don't know if he *is* alive,' Kate whispered to Charlie as he wrapped a thermal blanket around the two of them.

'Well, let them think he is,' Charlie cautioned. 'It's what everyone needs right now.'

An army vehicle arrived and she was bundled into it, the baby still tucked against her skin.

She'd have to give him up soon and examine him properly, or let someone else do it, someone not so terribly, terribly tired.

Someone she didn't know took him gently from her, and someone else she didn't know guided her towards the mess.

'A hot drink, food?' the kind stranger asked, and Kate shook her head.

'Just a bed," she said. 'Nothing more.'

CHAPTER EIGHT

How long she'd slept she didn't have a clue, but she awoke to noise and bustle all around the makeshift camp, voices yelling instructions, motors revving.

She sat up, slowly and experimentally, small movements while still prone suggesting she might be stiff and sore.

Two words that hardly covered it, she realised as she bent over to unlace her boots.

Every muscle in her body ached.

A shower—that would help.

Somehow she managed to make it that far, pausing only to grab clean army-issue clothing as she passed their neat supply.

The shower helped—even to the extent she now realised she was hungry. From the noise and yelling outside she presumed they were packing up. She hoped they hadn't shut the mess tent yet.

She also hoped, shocked by her original selfish thought, that the movement meant everyone had been accounted for. Hoped the death toll hadn't been too great.

The mess was still where it should be but the big tent—Angus's tent—lay like a deflated balloon on the ground, a soldier Kate didn't recognise barking instructions about how it should be folded.

The tent!

It had brought Angus back into her life, if only briefly—and had brought a very special time with him as well. But this latest reunion—meeting again here—had been pure chance. And now he'd tested his tent in a disaster response situation, he'd be off far and wide—he and his tent. Taking it to wherever it was needed, like drought-stricken or war-torn villages in Africa or disease-riddled refugee camps in South East Asia.

She closed her eyes briefly, shutting out images of him in danger in some foreign land, and bumped straight into a broad chest.

'I was coming to check you weren't dead,' he said, steadying her with firm hands on her shoulders, sending messages she shouldn't feel right through her body.

'I'm fine, just starving,' she said. 'I was pleased to see the mess tent still standing.'

He smiled at her, although for some reason the smile, while kind, didn't quite reach his eyes, didn't crinkle the skin at the corners of them.

Because this was goodbye all over again?

Because their meeting up like this had been chance, nothing more, and the now was definitely over.

But he was speaking to her and she had to listen. Something about the mess tent always being the first one up and the last one down.

'Haven't you heard the term that an army marches on its stomach?'

She probably had, but it was *her* stomach troubling her.

Her stomach and something in Angus's manner.

Forget that, she muttered inwardly as she made her way towards the servery. His manner has nothing whatsoever to do with you!

'Did you hear how the baby is? Did he live?' she asked, when she realised he was walking beside her.

What she couldn't ask was had the baby been

alive. She really, really didn't want to think she'd failed to get there in time—failed to save him.

'The baby's fine,' he said, and to Kate's dismay tears began to leak from her eyes, sliding silently down her cheeks. Tears of relief, she knew—but unstoppable.

She felt a soft touch on the small of her back and a handkerchief pressed into her hand with an extra squeeze of her fingers. Angus's way of comforting her in the busy and no doubt gossip-rife mess.

She wiped her eyes but couldn't stop the tremors of relief that threatened to make a fool of her again.

'Find a seat, I'll bring food. And coffee?'

She nodded, and hurried to a seat beside one of the plastic windows, seeing, yet not seeing, all the activity outside.

'Bit late for breakfast, but I thought bacon and eggs were probably appropriate.'

Angus set down a tray on the corner of the table as he spoke and proceeded to lay out the table—knife and fork, coffee cup and pot, salt and pepper, and finally a covered plate, the cover lifted to reveal not only bacon and eggs but a small sausage and two pieces of grilled tomato.

Kate smiled up at him, still hovering by the table.

'That looks fantastic,' she said, and, although disconcerted by the now silent presence by her side, she began to eat, savouring each mouthful as the hot comfort food brought her slowly back to life—conscious life, real life.

Even if he wasn't sitting with her, this was probably the last meal she'd eat with Angus, so images of other meals they'd shared rose unbidden in her mind.

Tender salt and pepper squid in a little café in Manly, the fairy floss—hardly a meal—at Luna Park. They'd only had time for a coffee and tiny muffin at the art gallery—now bacon and eggs before he went away again.

She set down her cutlery, aware the lump in her throat would prevent her swallowing.

She looked up at the cause of all her problems—although, in truth, her loving him wasn't really *his* fault, especially when he'd warned her from the start that his career and marriage didn't mix.

'Aren't you even having coffee?' she asked.

'I should be outside, supervising things, but I wanted...'

He sounded hesitant, so unlike Angus she gestured to the chair opposite.

'Sit down, Angus. Sit down and tell me, although if it's anything to do with this meeting up again—about it not meaning anything, not being part of that "now" we had—then I already realise that.'

He sat so she could look at him—at this man she loved but couldn't have—and wondered if her own face looked as gaunt and troubled as his did.

She hoped not.

'So?' she prompted.

He spread his hands.

'It's hard to explain—the way the army works, that is—to someone not in it. It seems all ordered and regimented, which it has to be to move so many people around the place, continually training them, testing them, sending a group here, a group there. It would be chaotic if there weren't strict procedures and protocols and everyone in the army understands and obeys them.'

So, is this part of telling me why he can't see

me again, which I already know? Kate wondered, pushing her half-eaten breakfast aside, no longer the least bit hungry, the lump in her throat replaced by a knot in her stomach.

'But the thing the army does really well—really commits to—is making sure mail gets through. It's not so important now with email and texts and such but parents still write to their sons and daughters, lovers write to each other, and the army prides itself on getting the letters to the right person, no matter how long it takes. A kind of "the mail must get through" sentiment it's always had.'

Angus knew he was making a total mess of this, and the perplexed look on Kate's face reinforced this knowledge. But he'd been awake all night thinking about it, wondering, coming up with a dozen different scenarios, none of which were very satisfying or even plausible.

Then her tears earlier when she'd heard the baby was alive and she should have been happy—there were things going on that didn't add up. Did she regret not marrying the solicitor who'd cheated on her, regret not having a baby—a family—of her own? Or was it something to do with the deep inner sadness he'd sensed in Kate since meeting her again—a sadness he was sure hadn't been there on the island, for all she'd just cancelled her wedding?

And was he puzzling over this to delay bringing up the letter?

Because he wasn't sure how to approach her about it?

In the end, here at the table, he pulled the crumpled, much-redirected letter from his pocket and set it in front of them.

'I collected mail before I left the base, and only had time to go through it yesterday. Mostly rubbish and then this!'

He used one finger to push it across the table towards Kate, who had grown so pale he thought she might faint.

But she'd picked it up and looked at all the places it had gone to before it had finally reached him, touching each address.

'It partly took so long because letters are usually addressed to us by our ranks. Back then I was a captain so Dr Caruth probably didn't mean much to whoever sorted it. But the army, as you can see, is persistent.'

'Did you open it, read it?' she asked, in a voice so hesitant he barely heard the words.

'Of course,' he said, and waited.

And waited.

Until, perhaps realising she wasn't going to offer any explanation for the brief note he'd found inside the much-abused envelope, he said, 'You wanted me to phone you.'

If anything, she grew paler and her fingers on the envelope shook so much she put it down, steadying herself by flattening it against the table.

More silence, then she raised her head and looked directly at him.

'Not wanted so much, more just a suggestion.' Hesitated, then added, 'I really should be going—should find Blake and the rest of the team. If everyone's pulling out, I need a lift.'

She stood up, staggered a little, then straightened, and offered one of the most pathetic smiles he'd ever seen.

'It was good to see you again. I'm glad the tent worked.'

And on that note she marched steadily out of the mess.

Out of his life?

Again!

Not a request, a suggestion?

He pulled the straightened paper towards him and although he knew the words, he read them again.

Would you like to give me a call some time?
My number is 0623 348 876.

It still sounded like a request to him.

And why had it upset her so much that she'd virtually fled from his presence?

Embarrassment?

Confronted with it after so long?

Upset, even after all this time, over sending a note to someone who had been, as far as she'd known, about to be married?

He had no idea!

He shook his head, realising as he did it that women were largely foreign territory to him.

He'd known Michelle, or had thought he'd known her, yet hadn't realised just how much he'd hurt her by telling her about Kate. Kate had called him insensitive for telling, yet to him it had seemed the right thing to do—the honest thing to do. Yet looking back he wondered just how well he had known her, or understood the pain and fear she must have felt when he'd disappeared to who knew where.

And other women he'd dated, during times when Michelle had taken a break of her own, well, he'd never really been interested enough to try to work out what made them tick.

Pathetic!

That's what he was!

A great, big, pathetic lump of material, moulded by his training and the army into something very useful—someone who knew exactly what to do in any given situation in which he was involved.

But that was useful to the army, not a woman…

There was something he was missing here. He needed Gran with the common sense she'd tried to instil in him as a child, but she was long gone and no matter how hard he tried to figure out what advice she might give, he came up with a big fat zero.

Except Kate *had* sent the note.

He'd start from there…

Kate found the SDR helicopter as it was about to leave. Paul hauled her on board, whistling at her get-up, Blake saying he'd been about to send out a search party for her.

'I fell asleep,' she told them.

'Well, you deserved it. You were really amazing,' another team member said.

But the words of praise washed over Kate. The knowledge that Angus had her letter had shaken her so much she couldn't even begin to work out *how* to think about it, let alone what to think.

Surely it shouldn't matter why she'd written it. Not now—not after three years.

So why had he been so persistent?

Or had it been her own shock at seeing it that had made her think he'd been persistent?

Maybe he'd just been mildly interested.

Ha! That was about as likely as the moon being made of cheese.

She might not have known Angus long if you counted the time in hours and days, but she knew enough of him to know that he'd be like a terrier with a rat, refusing to let the matter go until he'd got to the bottom of it, however inconsequential it might be.

And she'd made it worse by not giving him an answer. She could have said something, any-

thing. Said it had just been a spur-of-the-mo-
ment thing. She'd forgotten all about it.

But she'd not only been too shocked to think
of anything to say, her reaction must have been
obvious to him from the glower he'd given her
before she'd departed.

She tried to put it out of her mind—wasn't
she already adept at that—but today little things
like the almost-not-there touch of his hand on
her waist as he'd guided her into the mess, the
strength of his fingers as he'd pressed a handkerchief into them had got to her.

Handkerchief!

She fished in her pocket and pulled it out. A
perfectly ordinary white square—fine linen,
she thought. Or good cotton, soft to touch but
firm at the same time.

She shook her head and jammed the offending scrap of material back where it belonged.
Was she losing it that she could sit here moon-
ing over a square of white linen?

Or cotton?

Pull yourself together, right now!

It was over, whatever it had been, and she
had exams looming so would need all her wits
about her when she got back to work.

Work had been her solace once before and it could be again—*would* be again.

Kate pulled the note out of her pigeonhole at the hospital a couple of days later. Saw the SDR initials in the corner of the envelope and wondered why the formality. Usually when anything was happening, Mabel phoned.

She opened and read it, realising as she did so that it wasn't a time and date for a regular SDR meeting but for a debrief for all those who'd been in the mountains.

Counsellors—that's what they'd be offering, she decided. That's why it's not a general meeting. Everyone was edgy about counselling—some certain they would never need it while others hated to admit they might.

Kate wondered if perhaps she might, whether it might help her sleep better, get through the night without dreams of Angus—Angus in danger, Angus touching her, Angus asking about the letter.

But it would be trauma counselling on offer rather than—

Well, *love* counselling!

She groaned, startling someone else checking for mail or notices. But this 'love' idea that kept popping into her head was really getting to her.

And what if it *was* love she felt for him? It wasn't as if she could do anything about it. He'd explained all that—explained any form of permanent relationship with him was out of the question.

So?

She checked the note. The meeting was an afternoon one, and as it was in the middle of her days off she'd certainly be able to make it. No doubt Blake, or more probably Mabel, had arranged the time for when most of the team who'd gone south *would* be available.

Kate knew the mother and baby were doing well, as the newspapers seemed to be carrying regular reports on their health status.

Apart from that...

Angus returned to Western Australia to finish his business there, and with that sorted, he only needed the debrief with the USAR and SDR teams who'd attended the recent operation before giving the go-ahead for production.

He was reasonably sure there'd be some new ideas to improve it.

He'd received a text from Mabel alerting him to the date and time of the meeting, and later a note advising him that three of the USAR team would also be there.

But would Kate?

Or would she find some excuse not to come, not wanting to meet up with him in case he asked more questions?

Perhaps the note she'd sent had meant nothing more than it had said—*give me a call some time*.

Had the fact that he hadn't called disappointed her? Hurt her in some way that even now she didn't want to talk about it?

He didn't think so—their time together had been short, but he was absolutely certain she wouldn't hold a grudge, not about something as trivial as a missed phone call anyway.

Which left him ready for this debrief with more than usual excitement. True, he'd be hearing the first reports on his tent from people who had actually used it in an emergency situation but, even better, he'd see Kate again.

See her when she wasn't exhausted and

overwhelmed by all she'd been through in the mountains.

But would she talk to him?

He'd made such a huge production of their relationship not being a relationship in the usual sense because he could be called away any time and be gone for weeks or months—maybe even for ever if it was a war zone.

And the last thing he'd wanted to do was hurt her—to hurt Kate as he'd hurt Michelle—coming and going without a thought for how she must feel about it.

He'd pushed the 'just for now' idea hard with Kate, and he was sure she'd been happy to go along with it.

Because it had suited her as well?

He stopped thinking about it all at that point, mainly because he didn't want to consider she hadn't cared enough to want more than 'now'.

Not when, after a few short days, he'd known for certain that he did.

Had known that he loved her—for all the good that would do him.

He groaned, then looked quickly around in case someone might have heard him.

* * *

Kate was shocked that she hadn't figured out Angus would be at the meeting. She'd been so certain it would be about counselling that she hadn't considered the obvious.

His tent had been on trial, its first actual deployment on a rescue mission. Of course he had to be there!

She'd just have to avoid him, that was all.

But if he asked again about the note she'd sent...

Perhaps she could lie.

Lie to Angus?

No way!

She couldn't lie to anyone—was a hopeless liar at the best of times—but with something so personal...

'You with us, Kate?'

Blake's voice brought her out of the futile arguments going on inside her head. He was doing a roll call—he always did a roll call so Mabel could make a note of who was present.

She waved her hand to let him know she *was* present, and proceeded to focus on the meeting.

All thoughts of the note were shoved aside as

she concentrated on Blake's summary of what they'd done.

The main representative of the USAR summarised their work before beginning a long discussion with Angus.

'It was the inflatability of your tent,' he said, and Kate smothered a smile. 'It had me wondering if we aren't underutilising air power, say, to provide safe tunnels through debris.'

And as Kate listened to the pair of them, others present adding suggestions or asking questions, she realised just how important sessions such as these really were because, with everyone sharing their expertise, new and safer ways of providing services would come into being.

Blake eventually diverted the meeting back to the suitability of the tent as a triage and emergency centre. Sam made a suggestion about the placement of surgical instruments, and it was Blake who answered, looking to Angus as he finished for a confirming nod.

And after thank yous had been said, and the reminder for counselling, the meeting broke up, Kate saying goodbye to Charlie from the

USAR team and nodding to most of the others as she headed for the door.

Where Angus had been caught by the USAR man, wanting more information about the tunnels he was hoping might work.

So it was the USAR man, not Angus, who touched her on the shoulder, asking her to wait a minute.

'Kate,' he said, 'you were down there having to get through to the injured woman, and later to the baby. Do you understand what I mean about some kind of protection around a rescuer in that kind of situation?'

Kate nodded, kind of including Angus in the nod.

'I don't understand enough about aerodynamics if that's what it is that keeps things inflated. And, yes, I think we'd all like more protection in hairy situations, but you have to look at it against cost. I don't know about USAR but the SDR is always looking for extra funds. And even more important is time. How long would it take to get something like that operational twenty or thirty feet below ground level? We needed to get that woman out fast.'

The USAR man nodded, but she could see he wanted more information from Angus, so she said goodbye to the two men and walked away, every nerve in her body conscious of Angus behind her.

CHAPTER NINE

THE MEETING HAD been held on the ground floor of the sprawling six-storey building, which meant Kate hadn't realised it was raining until she stepped outside.

And not just raining but pelting down, thunder rolling ominously somewhere to the west, lightning flashing across the grey sky.

She'd be soaked on the way home in this downpour!

Was there an umbrella in her locker? One she'd left there accidentally some time ago?

Her old parka—that would help.

Or maybe she could just get wet.

'Walk you home?'

She turned to see Angus just outside the foyer of the staff entrance, a huge umbrella held above his head, his face unreadable in its shadow.

Probably unreadable anyway, was her instant thought, knowing exactly why he was here and what he wanted to know. Although that knowledge didn't stop a huge skip in her heartbeat.

But nearly a week of sleepless nights and long discussions with herself during her runs hadn't resolved the dilemma in which she found herself.

Although it wasn't really a dilemma, was it?

He wanted to know and she would have to tell him.

She would tell him as concisely and unemotionally as she could.

The concise bit was okay. It was the next part that might be difficult.

Would be difficult.

Thanks,' she said, wondering if she'd taken an age to reply or if it had only seemed that way to her.

She stepped under the shelter of his umbrella and the simple act of sharing it with him, pressing close against him to avoid the rain, made her forget all the rational reasoning that had, only seconds earlier, gone on in her head.

Right now, she wanted nothing more than to be close to him.

Like this!

For whatever reason!

And for ever?

Did he feel the same that he didn't speak, simply putting his hand in the small of her back and guiding her towards the apartment block?

Except he didn't *do* for ever—he'd told her that…

But remembering the question he wanted answered banished the little dart of pain that thought brought in its wake.

But Alice would surely be home, so she, Kate, might be saved the question.

For now.

They reached the entrance and it was only polite that she ask him in.

'That'd be great,' he said, as if they hadn't ever been more than casual acquaintances— had never spent hot, steamy, and yet sometimes languorous, hours in bed. Never talked until their throats were dry, on ferries, and out walking, in restaurants, and on the Ferris wheel at Luna Park.

'Coffee?' she asked when they were safely inside, his umbrella dripping water on the balcony.

The word came out as a squeak, her nerves so tense it was a wonder she could breathe.

'Lovely,' he said, settling himself into an armchair for all the world as if he belonged in the apartment, not her.

But making coffee gave her time to calm down, to settle her unruly nerves, and calm the inner longings being close to him had generated.

It was only as she set some shortbread on a small plate and carried the tray out of the kitchen that she realised finally that Alice wasn't there. Closed her eyes briefly when she remembered it was Alice's charity shop day.

She waited until he'd picked up his coffee, surreptitiously studying him when she could.

Got nothing!

Not a hint of what he might be thinking or feeling.

Nothing.

Which meant she'd have to bring it up, because there was no other reason he could be here. Their 'now' time was over, she'd understood that was all it could be right from the start.

And the fact that it had been cut so short had reinforced the impermanence of their...

Relationship?

Hardly.

More a fling.

'I was pregnant!'

Suddenly the words were out there, not that difficult to say after all, but from the disbelieving look on Angus's face—or maybe it was shock—it wasn't what he'd expected to hear.

He set his coffee cup unsteadily down on the table and stared at her.

'When I wrote the note,' she added, because now she'd started she just wanted to get it over with. 'It was a shock. I'd been on the Pill, then with the cyclone and all the huts getting flattened, I had missed a few, and then I was back home and that's when I realised.'

She should stop now, let him speak, but there was more she had to say—to explain—for all she felt like curling into a ball and crying herself to sleep.

She swallowed hard.

'At first I couldn't decide what I'd do, but then I knew I wanted to keep it and I thought if I was doing that you had a right to know.'

You can do this, she told herself, just tell it as it was, the practical stuff.

'Just to know, not to help me or to put pressure on you. I knew I'd be okay financially and I could afford to take some time off, and then there'd be childcare but I could work part time so I could be with him as much as possible.'

Deep breath—nearly there—only now the memory of telling her parents and their immediate reaction—get an abortion—had returned to throw shadows over her words, so her voice, as she continued, wavered just a little.

'I had it all worked out but thought I should probably tell you, so that's why I wrote the note.'

Kate sat back, biting her lip, tense—with fear—when she should have been pleased with herself for getting it all out into the open without the hint of a tear or a shading of self-pity.

'And when I didn't phone?'

The words sounded as if he'd strangled them on the way out, but he was probably shocked.

It hurt! Kate thought but didn't say.

She closed her eyes, back in that time, but after a moment found the strength to answer.

'I felt you'd drawn a line under what had happened, and I honestly believed that was for the best. I didn't want it mucking up your and Michelle's marriage, either with guilt if you didn't tell her, or an extra child somewhere on the outer edges of your lives if you did.'

He sat in silence, staring at her as if he didn't know her, disbelief written clearly on his face.

Kate sipped her coffee, holding her cup in two hands in the hope he wouldn't notice she was shaking. She'd done her part and answered his question. Now she hoped like hell he wouldn't take it further.

She didn't handle the further very well.

Except he would—he'd have to really. Even now he was looking around the apartment as if to find a child she'd hidden somewhere. Or even a toy, a hint of a child...

'You miscarried?' he asked at last.

Kate shook her head.

'If only it had been that straightforward,' she said, standing up and walking to the long glass door that led onto the balcony, looking out over the streets awash with rain.

Angus tried to figure out that statement. If only it had been that easy? What the hell did she mean!

Damn it all, he'd run the whole gamut of emotions in the last few minutes and his brain wasn't working all that well, but surely he should be able to figure out...

Something hot was stirring inside him. He'd felt a jolt of it when she'd told him she'd been pregnant—she'd been pregnant with his child and he hadn't known. Yes, that had started the fire.

But this!

What he was thinking now!

He stared at her—at her straight back turned away from him, no doubt concerned about his reaction.

And so she should be!

'You had my child adopted?'

The heat propelled the words out far more sharply than he'd intended, and he saw her swing to face him.

'He was *my* child, and he was stillborn!' She flung the words at him, matching his anger with some of her own.

The enormity of what she'd said—the realisation of what she must have gone through—doused his anger faster than a cold shower. He stood up, walked across to where she was once again facing the window.

Put his arm tentatively around her waist, and

very slowly drew her to him, turning her so she stood in the shelter of his arms, holding her loosely until she all but fell against him and he could wrap his arms more tightly now and feel the shudder as she let go of the tension she had to have been feeling.

The pain she must have suffered was unimaginable and all he could do was hold her, rocking her slightly, hoping his body might tell her things his mind couldn't put into words.

She pushed away—not immediately—and returned to where she'd been sitting on the sofa.

Could he sit beside her?

Should he?

Realising there were so many more questions he wanted to ask, he went back to where he'd been sitting and finished his coffee, which wasn't cold but close.

'Can you talk about it? Do you want to?' he asked, and she frowned at him, confused.

'The baby,' he prompted. 'Did you find out what had happened? Did anyone give you a reason?'

'No, and no,' she said at last. 'It wasn't an obvious umbilical cord related death and although there have been numerous studies done through examination of the placenta, they rarely tell us anything constructive. The experts talked about placental insufficiency and foetal death syndrome but they were just words and what it all boils down to is that, apparently, it just happens.'

It was Angus's turn to get to his feet, needing to move, to pace the room, trying desperately to get a grasp on Kate's situation at the time. For all those months she'd been expecting this child, looking forward to its—his, she'd said—arrival, then suddenly there had been nothing. The pain, the tragedy of it was hard, almost impossible to comprehend. No wonder she'd changed, shut herself away from people, become, as someone had said, a loner.

He paced some more, still trying to get his head around it, more questions bubbling in his mind.

Would she answer them?

She was sitting there, so he knew she was still reliving it and he'd brought it all back to her—brought back her pain.

He sat beside her, put his arm around her shoulders and drew her close.

'Kate, I am so, so sorry, not only for not being

there for you at the time but for bringing it all back up now. I can only imagine how much it must hurt to have to talk about it. How it must take you back.'

She rested her head on his shoulder. 'It's not the first time I've been back there,' she said quietly, 'and every time I imagine a different outcome.'

He hugged her closer.

'Do you want to talk about it?' he asked. 'I'll stop now if you don't.'

He felt her head shake and heard a quiet, 'Of course you want to know. I don't mind.'

He moved so he could look at her, see her face, though his hand still rested on her shoulder.

'Did you know? Before the birth, I mean.'

She nodded.

'Only at the end.'

'And they did a Caesar?'

Headshake and a wry smile.

'Believe it or not, many obstetricians, including mine, believe a natural childbirth is better in such instances. They believe you get over it more quickly—no scar to heal then keep reminding you, or some such twaddle. I was too numb to argue so just went ahead.'

'On your own?'

She smiled—a better smile this time.

'I was in Brisbane, and not totally friend-less. I had good support, although my parents wanted nothing to do with any of it. They were so against my keeping it, cut me off completely. But in one way the obstetrician was right—I was back at work within a week and that was the very best part of all. It gave me time to think of other things and that's when I began to apply to join a surgery programme. I joined the Brisbane SDR as well, and life went on.'

Angus closed his eyes, imagining not just the death of a child but the death of someone you'd spent nine months getting to know, a little bit of yourself you'd probably talked to every day, bought supplies for, longing for his arrival. He could feel Kate's pain in his heart.

Then the knowledge that it had been his child struck him once more, and he felt the loss as though he'd been there, felt the pain in his own heart, had to do something—comfort her, feel her comfort himself...

Had to do something to make things right between them.

Something.

Anything!

He tightened his arms around her body, moving so they rocked together.

'Marry me,' he said, shocking himself when the words burst out yet suddenly knowing they were right—that it was what he wanted. To marry this woman he loved and had probably loved for the last three years.

And *that* knowledge added further shock!

But he wasn't as shocked as Kate, who sprang away from his sheltering arms.

'Marry you? Now, there's a bolt from the blue! Why ever would you want to marry me?'

'We had a child,' he said, still numb from all the revelations. His head was still trying to deal with his totally bizarre—not to mention inexplicable—suggestion. 'Shouldn't that count?'

'A child who died,' Kate reminded him bluntly. 'There *is* no child and no reason whatsoever to get married. Didn't you spend considerable time and energy telling me all the reasons you couldn't or wouldn't get married, all the stuff about never being here for a family, for your wife and children? I didn't tell you about the baby so you'd feel sorry for me, but because you asked me—kept asking me. And now you know, and nothing's really changed in either of our lives, and we can go our separate ways.'

He got to his feet and resumed pacing, something she'd seen him do before, and seeing the disbelief on his face, reading his consternation in the way he paced, her heart went out to him. She wanted to stand up, hold him in her arms, tell him everything would be all right.

But would it be?

The news she'd just given him had brought on the pain she'd lived with for the past two years—more now. Wouldn't he be feeling at least a little of that pain?

'I need to think. I'll go now,' he said suddenly, as if the room had become too small to hold his need to move.

So now she did hold him, putting her arms around him and saying gently, 'I know you have to take it in, but once you have, put it behind you, don't let it affect your life the way I've let it affect mine. I've got beyond that now, thanks to meeting you again, having that time together, short though it was. I'm moving forward, and you will too.'

A quick kiss, then she opened the door for him, trying hard to avoid the dark eyes that held shadows she recognised from the eyes she'd seen in her mirror for two long years.

He had a child—he'd *had* a child. This thought was caught up in a mix of battling emotions—anger that he hadn't known, resentment that Kate hadn't told him, pain for what she'd been through.

And loss.

That emotion overwhelmed them all, although it was stupid, pointless, if not downright nuts to feel a loss for a child he'd never had—never known he was going to have.

But loss was definitely there.

A child.

A son...

Had she given him a name?

What had he looked like?

About to turn, to go back to the apartment, Angus stopped himself in time. He'd already put Kate under tremendous strain, forcing this story out of her, and he couldn't make it worse.

So, back to the base where he should have gone an hour ago—straight from the debriefing—so he could type up the notes he'd made and think about the suggestions he'd heard.

On the whole, the tent had been a spectacular success, and although this should bring him joy, or at least pleasure, all he felt was flat—empty—bereft...

CHAPTER TEN

KATE GOT BACK to work—normal work—busy in Theatre, studying and surprising herself and her supervisor, Nick Warren, when she topped the state in the second-year surgical exams.

'Are you sure you don't want to specialise in a narrower field than general surgery?' he asked her. 'Orthopaedics offers the widest range, because you can choose just about any part of the body you want—hand, knees, backs, necks.'

She smiled at him.

'You don't need to keep naming skeletal parts I could study because, honestly, general surgery suits me just fine. I enjoy that I can work in the ED because there I do a little bit of everything. An open break in an arm doesn't always need a consultant orthopod called in—in fact, a nurse could probably do it—but I might be doing that one day, then some stitching of a wound another day, and sometimes cutting down to remove infection from a penetrating wound. It's the variety that keeps me going, Nick.'

'Well, it's how surgery started and there'll always be a need for general surgeons so you'll always have a job.'

He hesitated for a moment, then said, 'You *are* happy here? You're not thinking of leaving? You could get a job anywhere, I'm sure you get offers.'

Only one totally absurd one of marriage, prompted by shock, and that for all the wrong reasons, Kate thought as she assured Nick she had no intention of leaving.

'I just wondered,' he said. 'One of the big bosses, Justin Alexander—have you met him?'

Kate shook her head.

'It's just that he was asking about you and I thought you might have put in for a transfer or something, that he was interested. But it was probably just that you'd done so well in your exams.'

'I've never heard of him,' Kate said, although the name did ring vague bells.

'You probably wouldn't have. He's come across from North Shore. He's one of the pen-pushers these days, an administrator, although he was a top O and G man in his day.'

An administrator?

Angus's uncle?

Had Angus spoken of her to his uncle—to any of his family?

Surely not!

Kate turned the conversation to other things, the upcoming operations they had scheduled, in which ones she'd be the lead surgeon, anything special she'd need to know.

But as she walked home, she thought about the interest of a man called Justin Alexander and felt a little uneasy that people she didn't know might be discussing her.

Not about the baby—she was sure Angus wouldn't have passed that on.

But the conversation had left her head feeling muddled. She'd almost succeeded in clearing most of Angus out of it, packing him tidily away in yet another box, and now this! One of the powers-that-be discussing her with her supervisor.

It made her feel uncomfortable, to say the least.

She'd go home, change her clothes and go

for a run. A little sit in the cemetery, a chat to Joshua, and life would right itself.

Except it didn't.

Joshua had nothing to offer her so she rested a while, looking out to sea, watching a tanker move at what, from the distance, seemed like a snail's pace towards Botany Bay.

Harriet's arrival at what Kate considered 'her' place surprised her, especially as she'd heard the camera clicking and guessed she'd been photographed.

But Harry?

Here?

'You're out and about?' she said, unable to hide the surprise in her voice.

'Thanks largely to you and the photography suggestion,' Harry said with a smile. She held up the camera. 'You've made a monster of me, I'm completely hooked, and looking for new places to photograph has strengthened my leg no end.'

'That's great,' Kate told her, the shine in Harry's eyes telling her as much as the words.

'Of course, I'm still limping along like a three-legged dog, but you got me out and I've been meaning to thank you, but you're either rescuing babies in the Snowy or working all hours in Theatre so I haven't had a chance.'

She lifted the camera and snapped another shot.

'This place is magical—so much history here. You talked about the ocean in all its many moods, and this place is the same. I came here one day in the rain and I reckon got some of my best shots.'

Kate had to smile. Alice had pushed her into seeing Harry, and inadvertently she'd done some good.

But Harry had had another visitor that night and, remembering, Kate had to look away lest Harry saw her pain.

'I've got to get back,' she said, standing up and stretching. 'Great to see you out and about.'

Then she fled, running from her memories, afraid she'd never be fast enough to really escape them.

Without consciously realising it, Kate curled herself back into the protective shell she'd grown over the last couple of years. Missing drinks with the SDR team after meetings, saying no to Charlie when he phoned to ask her out, making her work and study her whole life.

But now she was more aware of the emptiness of it and the hollowness inside her. Aware she should do something about it but unable to try.

So she almost welcomed the phone call from Mabel, although she knew it meant people were in danger of some kind. But it brought a jolt of adrenalin that stirred her back to life.

Hostage situation in the nearest shopping centre—armed gunman, reports of shooting, specialist police units in charge and the SDR tasked with helping the injured, stabilising those who needed it before passing them on to the ambos, hospitals all over Sydney already on alert for victims.

The gunman was on the second-floor balcony that ran around the centre and shooting down towards people in the main food court below. The police and the building security men and women were trying desperately to evacuate the centre, but panicking people didn't take orders well.

To Kate and the SDR team, it looked about as easy as herding chickens, although most of their attention was on the wounded, lying on the floor, several of the injured slumped on the escalator, which had either jammed or was now turned off.

'We have to get out there,' she said to Sam, who was standing beside her in the little shelter offered by a pillar. 'Those people need attention.'

'The police are bringing in a negotiator,' Sam told her. 'Maybe they'll ask him to stop shooting so we can get to the injured.'

It was then Kate saw the child, obviously separated from her mother, now wandering past the shops on the first floor, crying quietly.

'He wouldn't shoot a child!' Sam said, catching sight of the little girl at the same time.

'But we don't know that,' Kate argued. 'You stay here, I'll go back to the food court and see if I can get to the child from there before she wanders into his line of fire.'

'Blake said remain under cover,' Sam reminded her.

'The far end of the food court is under cover—he can't see it from where he is. Besides, his attention is on the escalators in case someone tries to come up.'

She sidled, careful step by careful step, back into the shadows, keeping the pillar between her and the gunman. If she could reach the food court without being seen she knew there was an elevator towards the rear of it, and with any luck could get to the little girl before she moved into sight on the floor below him. But the gunman was wary and his peripheral vision would catch the slightest movement.

The plan fell to pieces when the elevator pinged on reaching the first floor, and although she couldn't see the gunman on the floor above she could tell from the cries of the people trapped below her that he'd moved, while a shrill scream suggested he'd taken a hostage.

But Kate's attention was focussed on the child. Slipping from shadowed doorway to doorway, she realised that part of the centre's plan must have been to close all the shops and dim the lights. The child's mother was probably behind one of those closed doors.

She reached the child and lifted her, but was uncertain what to do next.

Which way had the gunman moved—to the left or right? Choosing the wrong direction could bring Kate and the child into his sights.

So she stayed where she was, sitting down in a darkened doorway, talking quietly to the little girl. And tried to think what had been decided after an enquiry into another hostage crisis in the city some years earlier.

Were specialist army personnel coming in to handle things, or had the police devised a new protocol for dealing with these situations?

Either way, Kate was content to stay where she was, certain all the businesses would have rear exits and as many people as possible would have been evacuated when the shooting had begun.

She couldn't see the negotiator but heard him introducing himself through a bullhorn. Talking to the gunman, quietly and calmly.

The gunman's response was a new barrage of bullets, and now Kate held her hands over the little girl's ears, although she doubted that would help.

So she talked, quietly, about birds and animals, about family and friends, rocking the child in her arms as she rattled on.

'And just what do you think you're doing here?' a far-too-familiar voice whispered angrily in her ear.

'Where did you come from,' she demanded, as quietly as her shock would allow.

'I was at the hospital to talk to Blake about joining the SDR team,' he said. 'Sam told me where you were.'

'The child was wandering around this balcony looking for her mother, she'd have come into his line of sight within minutes,' she explained, while the 'I'm at the hospital to talk to Blake about the SDR' comment he'd made snagged somewhere in her head but was making no sense at all.

'We're quite safe,' she told him, adding, 'or at least we were until a great hulking man appeared and we had to share our shelter.'

Angus ignored her protest, instead settling himself on the floor beside her and the child, his back against the door of the closed shop.

'Who's handling it?' Kate asked, assuming the army given that Angus was here.

'Specially trained police squad. They're moving men in through the rear doors and will come through the shops and get him.'

'Not kill him?' Kate asked, feeling there'd been enough bloodshed.

'Only if they have to,' Angus told her, adding, 'Did you miss the bit about me talking to Blake about joining the SDR team?'

She turned to peer at him in the gloom.

'You're what?'

'Quiet,' he whispered, holding a finger to her lips and sending such a jolt through her body it was a wonder she still held the now sleeping child.

'What do you mean about joining the SDR team? *Our* SDR team?' she whispered back at him, tension adding anger to her words.

'Just that!' he said. 'Mind you, I'm exaggerating slightly. It takes a while to get out of the army but, looking ahead, I was at the hospital talking to Blake today when the call went out, and I thought I might as well come along. Though not in time to stop you putting yourself in danger.'

Kate shook her head. Nothing he'd said made any sense to her, but she doubted this was the time to be considering it. Right now they needed to stay safe—to keep the child safe.

She could hear the negotiator still talking, although Angus's whispered words had all but blotted the negotiations out.

Now it was her thoughts making it difficult to understand him.

But something must have happened because black-clad men—and possibly some women—heavy with bullet-proof gear—were carrying the injured swiftly into the shadows on the ground floor, while muted sounds from above suggested another group was approaching the man.

The negotiator kept talking, and Kate realised he was distracting the man's attention and possibly using the noise of the bullhorn to cover the slight movements on the second floor.

It was only later that evening that Kate saw what had happened on the news channel, five men converging on the gunman and putting him on the ground, relieving him of his weapon, searching and then handcuffing him, finally leading him away to a waiting police van.

In the shopping centre, someone had yelled the all-clear and chaos had erupted as people who'd been separated during the evacuation searched for their friends or relations, oblivious to police commands to remain calm and seek police help in their search.

Angus had disappeared as silently as he'd approached and Kate wondered if he'd been a dream, although his whispered words still jangled in her head. Had he really said something about getting out of the army?

But why?

She found a frantic mother and reunited her with her child, both of them in tears, and went looking for whatever members of the SDR team who might still be around.

Sam and Paul were by the van that they used in the city and she returned to the hospital with them.

'Blake went to the hospital with a critically injured man,' Sam explained. 'He'd lost a lot of blood because of the stand-off. If we could have got to all those injured faster than we did, there'd have been less chance of anyone dying, but as it is this man and a younger woman are both listed as critical. Kate, you've been in SDR longer than I have, is there any training for this kind of thing? Can we as a response team do more?'

Kate thought about it, then said, 'I don't think so. We all have our roles in these crises, although that's the first hostage situation I've been in. But generally speaking the police have jurisdiction, especially in the city, and they have an elite squad that responds. A special squad from the army is the next lot called in, along with the fire and ambulance services— or maybe they come before the army. But we're there to treat the injured and in things like mass shootings there could be plenty of those.'

'Too many to be worrying about other aspects of the situation?' Sam said, and Kate nodded.

But once back at the hospital it was hard to settle into work, with images of Angus, and whispers of the strange things he'd said, foremost in her mind.

The page requesting her presence in the ED came as a relief. She really didn't want to be operating on anyone without her mind one hundred per cent on the job.

Down there, it soon became clear that most of the damage was collateral. People cut by broken glass when a shot had shattered a shop window, others injured by flying masonry chipped from a wall near them by a bullet.

Several people had been hurt in the panic to get to safety, and all in all the place was chaotic.

The nurse at the triage desk saw Kate walk in.

'Cubicle twelve,' she said. 'Cuts from flying glass.'

Kate moved towards the cubicle—the curtained room providing some privacy but certainly not soundproof, which was how she couldn't avoid hearing a deep, familiar voice from the cubicle next door.

Undoubtedly Angus, which made as little sense as his earlier SDR conversation.

But she had a patient, the clothes the woman had been wearing already replaced with a gown, and on a drip to replace blood loss, provide pain relief and mild sedation, but the woman's wounds were from more than flying glass.

'Someone pushed me through a window,' she said weakly, and, lifting protective cotton pads on her arms and legs to see the damage, Kate knew it would be a long job.

She looked at the nurse assisting her.

'We'll need to flush every wound very carefully to see there's no glass embedded in it. Some we can close with strips but others will need stitches. Could you start that while I check that none of them are bleeding badly enough to be treated immediately? If not, we'll start at the top and work down.'

Kate checked all the wounds, irrigating them as she worked, pleased that they were mostly shallow.

But the face was important. She didn't want to leave the woman scarred for life—a permanent reminder of a terrifying time.

Together, they washed and stitched and dressed the woman's wounds, Kate especially careful to minimise any scarring.

'So this is what general surgery is all about,' a voice said quietly, and Kate froze for a moment, before turning to see Angus, dressed as she was in bloodied scrubs.

A thousand questions rattled in her head, not one of which she could ask right now. Instead she had to concentrate on her patient, giving her all her attention, so distractions like her body's reaction to Angus had to be hastily slapped down,

'I might see you later,' he said.

'What's he doing here?' she asked the nurse when she'd tied off the last stitch in her patient's cheek.

'Something about joining the ED in the near

future—checking the place out,' the nurse replied. 'Gorgeous, isn't he?'

Too gorgeous for his own good, Kate thought, but as the nurse's explanation left her more bamboozled than ever, she ignored it too.

Somehow she got through the day, although an eight-hour shift had turned into fourteen hours, with brief stops for coffee and food to keep her going. She had admitted the woman with the myriad glass cuts, wanting her kept on IV antibiotics for a few days in case there was any infection.

The woman's husband was with her when Kate came to check on her patient before leaving the hospital, profuse in his thanks for all she'd done.

'Visiting hours are over so I'll walk out with you,' he said, and she stepped outside while he said goodbye to his wife, waiting because she sensed he wanted to talk to her.

'Will the wounds heal?'

The question burst from his lips when they were only yards from the ward.

'They will,' Kate assured him.

'But completely? No scars?'

Kate shook her head, suddenly exhausted, but the man was concerned so she had to explain.

'Can we grab a coffee? It's only machine stuff and any resemblance to coffee is purely accidental but I need a hot drink and we can sit in the visitors' chairs and drink it while we talk.'

He hurried to get them both a cup of weak, warm liquid, carrying both to a small seating area by the elevators.

She took a sip, grimaced, but forced a little more down.

'She's had multiple injuries, but it's mostly shock we're worried about now. Some of the deeper cuts may leave scars but I'm reasonably certain her face will be okay. Some scars will leave faint white lines for a while, but nothing that can't be covered by a fine film of make-up.'

The man gave a sigh of relief.

'It's not that she's vain or anything, but she always looks after herself. She goes to the gym, only eats the right foods and looks after her skin. She'd be devastated if she was badly scarred.'

It was Kate's turn to sigh.

'You have to remember that they will look

bad at first—red and even puckered—but give it time, use the creams she'll be given when she leaves the hospital, and they should all end up minimal at the most.'

'Oh, thank you,' the man said, abandoning the coffee and getting to his feet, bending to give Kate a hug of gratitude before heading for the lift.

'Do all the men you meet give you thank-you kisses?'

Kate looked up to see Angus looming over her.

'Why are you here?' she asked, far too tired to explain what had just happened, and far too confused to work out what was happening with Angus.

'They told me in the ED you'd come up with your patient.'

She knew she was frowning.

'So?' she asked.

'I came to find you. I want to talk to you.'

'Oh, Angus, I am so tired I've been wondering if I'll make it home or if I can find a spare bed somewhere here to sleep, if only for a few hours.'

She studied him, trying to read the expression on his face.

Nothing there.

So she added, 'I'm really far too tired to talk about anything.'

'Then I'll walk you home.'

And talk even if I don't want to listen, Kate thought.

She shook her head.

'I'm going to find an on-call bed—there's sure to be a vacant one somewhere in the hospital. I just need to crash for a few hours. Can we talk later?'

Although did she really want to talk to him?

This thing about getting out of the army, maybe joining the SDR, stuff she'd heard in snatches today was making her feel very unsettled. Was it something to do with the Snowy situation? Did he feel his tent had failed?

Could he be doing it for her?

Surely not!

Just thinking about it made her feel worse.

'Tomorrow morning, breakfast. I'll meet you at Luigi's at seven.'

Kate bit back a groan and nodded, but as she got rather shakily to her feet, Angus was there, holding her elbow, steadying her, so close that, even exhausted, her body responded to his with all the usual fervour.

'Come on,' he said. 'I'll get a cab, see you home. You'll sleep better there.'

He took her home, asking the cabbie to wait while he went up to the apartment with her.

'You don't have to come in and undress me,' she said, as he took the key and unlocked the door for her. 'I'll go straight to bed.'

'You'd better,' he told her, then dropped a kiss on her lips and disappeared back along the corridor to the elevator.

Once inside, she showered and fell into bed, her mind wanting to go over the strange things that had happened that day—mainly the strange Angus things—but sleep claimed her immediately, a deep, dreamless sleep...

CHAPTER ELEVEN

KATE WOKE AT SIX. It was habit from as far back as school. And now if she was on duty at seven she had plenty of time to get ready, and if she wasn't on until nine she could go for a run first.

She was contemplating the run when something echoed in her brain—words—a meeting. Angus!

He wanted to talk and she was wary about the talk.

Slowly, the events of the day and the stray snippets of Angus stuff filtered back into her conscious mind.

It took a while to get out of the army—talking to Blake about the SDR—checking out the ED. Oh, hell! That explained her wariness, although surely he wouldn't be doing this because of her.

Please let it not be about her...

She loved him desperately but if he was doing

it for a wife and family—well, that made her stomach ache.

And the alternative that it might be about some other woman only made her feel worse.

She forced herself out of bed and dressed hurriedly.

Seven at Luigi's!

At least she'd find out.

Angus couldn't recall ever feeling this nervous, not even when mortar shells were exploding around him.

Nervous, *and* excited!

Everything was falling so neatly into place. Only this morning he'd had a text from Blake about an apartment in the building where Kate lived with Alice. Three bedrooms, up for sale—once owned by another Bayside doctor. He could move in and rent until the sale went through...

So why the nerves?

Because Kate had seemed a little strained last night?

But he could put that down to the long and traumatic day she'd had.

Kate!

He smiled to himself, pleased with all he'd managed to organise in such a short time.

He reached the café before her and found a quiet table on the pavement, looking out over the beach. Then there she was, walking towards him, not smiling—well maybe a small pretend smile—but she'd still be tired.

He stood up to greet her, took her in his arms to kiss her, felt her stiffen, turn a little so his kiss hit her cheek.

Tired?

She sat down, ordered coffee from the hovering waiter, then turned to him.

'So, talk!' she said, and Angus felt his throat tighten and his mouth go dry.

This wasn't how he'd planned it.

'We should get our breakfast order in before it gets too busy,' he said. 'We should tell the waiter when he brings the coffee.'

'One slice of banana bread toasted,' she said, and although he wanted to tell her she should eat more than that for breakfast, he had finally caught on that this was not the joyous reunion he'd somehow imagined.

He gave the orders, watched as she stirred sugar into her coffee and took a sip, looking at him over the rim of the cup, eyes making the same demand.

Talk!

'I don't know how much you took in of what I was saying yesterday. It was all so chaotic, and nothing definite's been organised yet, but—'

She put down her coffee, tilted her head to one side, and looked at him—really looked.

'Angus, start at the beginning. Start with the army.'

His hands seemed to be shaking so he put down his coffee cup. He'd have liked to reach out and take her hands in his but hers were still firmly wrapped around her cup.

'I'm getting out,' he said. 'I've done enough.'

'But your tent?' she protested. 'You wanted to go wherever it went. It was your dream from the very beginning.'

She sounded perplexed, which was understandable, although he had hoped for a little excitement...

'I've got others who know as much about it as I do. Now we know it works and with a few modifications after the Snowy experience I'll go to China where they'll manufacture them, but after that I'm free.'

'Free?'

Still perplexed!

'Free to take a job here at Bondi Bayside. Apparently, they've had locums working in the ED since someone called Luc Braxton left and the job's mine if I want it.'

Still no sign of excitement. He was starting to feel jittery. This wasn't going at all the way he'd planned.

Long silence, Kate studying him, expressionless now.

Then—

'Why are you doing this, Angus?'

She didn't know!

Couldn't guess?

Had he been mistaken about how she felt?

Had the love he'd been slow to recognise but was now strong enough to move mountains— and get out of the army—been one-sided?

That thought made him feel very hollow, so hollow he knew that answering, 'For you, for us,' would be a big mistake.

He took a deep breath.

'Finding out about the baby, it spun me off course. For days I felt…not lost but completely disoriented. For the first time in my life I didn't have a compass in my head telling me exactly what lay ahead. Yet I *did* know what lay ahead—things I'd spent what seemed like for ever planning, going with the tent wherever it was needed. Suddenly it wasn't enough.'

He paused, looking at her across the table, wondering if any of his words were making sense to her.

'I thought maybe it was because the tent had been successful and I needed a new project, or maybe the deaths down in the Snowy had affected me more than I'd thought. I haven't been much fun—a bear with a sore head had nothing on me as I mooched around the place, snapping at people who'd done nothing to deserve it, and generally making everyone around me miserable too. I was seriously considering counselling when I began to realise it wasn't me at all, it was the army.'

'The army?'

'Don't get me wrong, I love the army. It's been my life—my dream since I was a child—given me so much, but suddenly I knew I didn't belong there any more. It was time to leave,' he said firmly.

And that was true. He'd had enough of army life, and wanted something more, something settled, normal. And if he didn't find it with Kate—

He wouldn't go there.

Their breakfast arrived, just in time to ease the tension that had suddenly built like a thick cloud between them, but as he watched her butter her toast and cut it into neat squares his heart knew he wanted to see her do that again—and again—if possible every morning for the rest of their lives.

Kate picked up a small square of toast, not really wanting to eat it, sure it would taste like sawdust, she felt so uptight.

Angus hadn't said it, but she was reasonably certain that this whole idea of leaving the army and coming to work at Bayside was something he'd done for her.

And her heart ached inside her, that he would make such a sacrifice. No one who'd spent any time with Angus could help but know how much the army, and particularly his tent, meant to him.

He'd asked her to marry him, and she'd reminded him that he'd learned from past experience that the uncertainty of army life, particularly his army life, was too hard on relationships—too hard on a wife and children...

And if that was why he was getting out of the army then she, for all she loved him—because she loved him—wasn't the one for him.

But what could she say?

I love you but I won't marry you?

Too hurtful.

Make light of it?

Could she?

She ate another square of toast—sawdust.

Looked at a point just beyond his left shoulder and—well, gabbled really.

'Well, it seems as if you've got it all sorted. And if you come to Bayside it will be great to have you in the SDR! You can bring such a lot of different experience to it. I bet Blake was thrilled at the idea. And if you're replacing Luc in the ED his—'

Apartment was for sale at the moment.

That's what she'd been about to say when she'd realised that while working in the same hospital as Angus would be a permanent source of pain to her, having him living in the same apartment block would be sheer torture.

Especially when he found the wife and children...

But she, Kate, could get out of the SDR—her surgical work would be getting more extensive this year, less time in the ED. She could do this.

She risked a glance at him, but his head was bent over the enormous breakfast he had ordered.

His hair was a little longer, showing the curls that probably made him keep it short, and her fingers twitched with the urge to touch it, feel its softness, run her fingers through it. She watched his hands, cutting a sausage neatly and precisely, and remembered them sliding across her body, bringing it alive at the slightest touch.

And her body ached for him, ached to hold him, feel his warmth, his heat, to kiss him and be lost in his kiss, to lose herself in him—in love...

Angus ate with grim determination. Somehow, somewhere along the line, his careful planning had gone disastrously wrong. He'd heard Kate's words—had felt them like knife wounds, in fact—but they were...

False?

He ate another slice of sausage.

No, they hadn't rung false, yet *some* emotion had been there behind them.

And as if he'd take the offered job at Bayside, knowing she was working in the same hospital, being so close to her yet not hers— she not his...

He needed to get away, out of the café, go for a long walk, anything to clear his head, but he was damned if he'd leave his breakfast— damned if he'd let her see how upset he was by her casual brush-off.

Because that's what it was!

Or was it?

Something niggled at him.

Something whispering that there was more...

'I've got to go—on duty.'

She was on her feet, beside him, and he caught her hand.

'Kate?' he said, and looked up in time to see her squeeze her eyes shut, but not before he'd seen the sheen of tears.

'I'll see you around,' she said, oh, so casually, after which she retrieved her hand and walked away.

CHAPTER TWELVE

IT TOOK ANGUS five weeks to finalise his 're-turn to civvy street' plan, then suddenly he was there—in the ED, at SDR meetings and, worst of all, living in the same apartment block.

So how could she not walk home from work with him if they happened to leave the hospital at the same time?

For Kate, it was agony. All the memories she'd tried so hard to pack away had escaped, so her body hummed with inner excitement, her skin tightened at the slightest accidental touch, while his voice—though often she barely registered a word he said—filled her body with an aching longing she hadn't known existed.

Not that Angus felt any of these manifestations—not even awkwardness—prattling on as he would to any colleague about the new challenges he was finding in the job.

It was only after she'd changed shifts three times that she began to suspect these meetings, the walks home together weren't entirely accidental. Was he doing it to torture her?

Prove something?

She had no idea, but it was affecting her to the point that it was only by maintaining the strictest self-discipline that she could concentrate on work.

But once home, inside, she was a mess, distracted, picky, even short with Alice at times, wanting nothing more than to shut herself away in a dark hole and wait for the storm of emotions to go away.

Had Alice spoken to Harry that she came knocking on the apartment door on Kate's day off, finding Kate still in her pyjamas at ten o'clock?

'Not running today?' Harry asked, raising her eyebrows at Kate's attire, knowing that Kate ran every day she could—especially on days off.

'No!'

Simple answer, not exactly rude but fairly blunt.

'Because of Angus?' Harry, undeterred, continued.

'What the hell's it got to do with Angus?' Kate growled, and Harry smiled at her.

'You can't honestly believe that the entire staff of the hospital hasn't seen that something's up between you and Angus. I'm working in Geriatrics before I get back to ICU and it's even whispered about up there. Gorgeous new doc who'd tempted Kate Mitchell out of her shell, now working at the hospital and being ignored by said Kate while the sexual tension between the two of you could cause spontaneous combustion!'

'That's ridiculous,' Kate snapped, while her stomach clenched and unclenched.

'Is it?' Harry said gently. 'Kate, you gave me a prod when I was feeling too sorry for myself to be bothered with life. Now it's my turn. Even the most self-focussed member of the staff— and you know we get plenty of those—can see the sparks that fly between you and Angus. And anyone being caught between the two of you can feel the force field of whatever it is you share.'

She paused, obviously waiting for some input from Kate, but she was too flabbergasted by Harry's words to say anything at all.

'All I'm saying,' Harry carried on, 'is to at least explore the situation. Talk to the man, throw yourself into his arms, do something, anything, even if it's a risk, but don't let something as powerful as whatever's between you go to waste without at least giving it a go.'

Throw yourself into his arms?

Oh, how she longed to do that! One last time because surely it would lead to them making love. And in the languorous bliss after that she could explain—even tell him she loved him and then explain—and maybe after that she'd go back to Brisbane. He'd find someone else—

That thought was like a knife wound in her chest.

'Well?' Harry said, and Kate found a smile for her. Not a very good one, she was sure, but Harry had spoken out of kindness and friendship.

'Thank you,' Kate said, and she leaned forward and gave Harry a hug, walked her to the door and let her out.

But thinking Throw yourself into his arms was far easier than working out how to do it.

Except that Alice had gone back up to the island for an old staff reunion and she was alone in the flat.

Entice him in?

No, she had to be proactive.

Would he be at home?

His—Luc's—apartment was at the front of the building with the ocean view, so she couldn't see if lights were on or not.

So she'd visit!

But in her daggy pyjamas?

She smiled to herself, remembering the day he'd left her at the art gallery, suddenly called away. She'd gone to the Queen Victoria Building and as well as some fancy underwear she had bought a gorgeous nightdress, soft cream silk with a low V-neckline trimmed with lace and tiny rosebuds.

She'd meet someone in the corridor for sure if she paraded down to Angus's apartment in that, but if she wore her terry towelling dressing gown over it she could be popping down to borrow a cup of sugar from a neighbour.

More or less!

Her excitement was growing. She might be planning to say goodbye to Angus, but let it be a glorious goodbye.

She showered, used moisturiser and perfume, not too much, pulled on the slinky gown and shook her head.

What on earth was she thinking?

What if someone was there?

What if someone *from the hospital* was there?

She was about to take it off when the knowledge that this might be her last chance to lie in Angus's arms hit her with the force of a tidal wave.

Damn it all, she'd do it.

But she'd ring him first.

She dialled his number—fingers shaking on the keys—heard his deep 'Angus Caruth' and her courage faltered.

'Kate, is that you?'

Of course, her name had come up on his screen.

She drew a deep breath and then, oh, so casually, said, 'I just wondered if you were home. I could pop in. That's if you haven't any visitors.'

Long silence.

'No, no visitors,' he said, which wasn't exactly welcoming but she was too uptight to dither any more.

'I'll see you soon.'

She went swiftly down the corridor—it would have been too easy to turn back if she'd dawdled—and knocked on his door.

Given that Kate had barely spoken to him since he'd arrived at Bayside, Angus was already puzzled by the phone call, but opening the door to Kate, clutching a towelling dressing gown around her slim figure, he was completely thrown.

'Are you going to ask me in? Just for now?'

There was a quiver in Kate's voice that pierced the armour he'd begun to build around his heart, and he put his hands on her shoulders and pulled her gently towards him, shutting the door behind her.

And for a moment, it was enough just to have her in his arms again.

He had no idea what had gone wrong between them, let alone why his change of career had obviously upset her, but for now she was here.

So he kissed her, gently at first, then, as a tiny moan escaped her lips, his kiss drew harder, hotter, more demanding.

The thick towelling robe had fallen open and

underneath was fabric as smooth and soft as her silky skin.

'I should say wow but I doubt it will be on you long enough for me to truly appreciate it,' he said thickly, and heard her chuckle, felt it in her throat as he pressed kisses to the slim column of her neck and downwards, teasing at the deep V of the gown to find her breast, her nipple.

She wove her fingers in his hair and gave a gasp as he licked and nipped the thickened nub, then she was in his arms, the slinky material torturing him as he carried her to his bed, set her down on it and took in her beauty.

'Love me,' she whispered, and he needed no second bidding, stripping off his clothes to join her on the bed.

He kissed her. Teasing kisses at first, while his hand slid the soft fabric up her leg, his kisses more insistent as his fingers found her warmth. Then brushing tiny roses aside, he teased her nipple again, her fingers holding his head to her, wanting more yet squirming at his touch.

And when his lips claimed hers again, she took him in her hand and guided him into her, moving slowly at first as they adjusted to each other, before it became a race, a battle to be one, their bodies demanding more and more until finally they lay, depleted, joined and close, slick sweat warm on both their bodies...

Together.

And with her arms tight around him, his head resting on her breast, she began to talk, so softly and slowly he knew every word held tears.

'I love you, Angus. Love you more than I could ever imagine I could love anyone. But leaving the army, coming to Bayside. You should have said, we should have talked. I would have told you it was only ever going to be for the "now". Not this now but the "now" we had back then. That's what we'd agreed, and even when I knew I loved you, I felt at least I'd have that memory for ever.'

Angus heard the words, even understood them for they were simple English, but the meaning was eluding him, so he kept silent, waited, aware now that this was why Kate had come.

Oh, going to bed with him had obviously been a big part of it, but he saw now it had been her way to break down the walls that had risen between them.

Break them down so she could talk.

'You told me once you wouldn't marry because being married to an army officer in the job you did was no life for a wife and family. Some people obviously do it and do it well, but you felt with the tent and calls to dangerous or just disease-ridden places it was unfair to have someone waiting and worrying at home.'

She paused, held him closer, ran her fingers lightly over the planes of his face, kissed the top of his head.

'Then suddenly you're out of the army, working here, talking about a wife and children.'

Her voice cracked and he guessed they'd reached the heart of the conversation.

'What I hadn't said, hadn't told you,' she whispered, snuggling closer to him now, 'was that after the baby was stillborn, the specialist was doubtful I'd carry a live child to term. He had some garbled explanation but I wasn't listening because I didn't ever want to go through what had happened again, determined I wouldn't—couldn't. Not all that waiting and the caring and excitement and then nothing but a huge hole in my heart and aching, empty arms...'

He eased away, seeing clearly now. This woman he loved and who definitely loved him backing off because he'd been foolish enough to talk about a wife and children—a family— the children part being the barrier that had grown between them.

He propped himself on his elbow and looked down at her, traced her lips with his thumb.

'Did you honestly believe I'd turn my back on you—find someone else to marry—because you might not be able to give me children? Did you think I was so shallow that some vague idea of family would make me reject you?'

He heard his voice, knew it was harsh, but would have continued had he not seen the tears on her cheeks. And with aching heart he gathered her into his arms and held her tight, rocking her as he would a crying child, the love he felt for her enveloping them both.

'My darling Kate. It's you I love, just you. Yes, should we happen to have a child I'd love it too, but, no matter what, I love you. And anyway I don't believe the pundits who told you such rotten news, probably when you were very vulnerable. I've read up on stillbirths, mainly to gain an idea of even a fraction of the pain you must have gone through, and for pregnancies where there might be problems, there are now foetal monitors the mother can wear in the last trimester, and with any hint of the foetal heartbeat faltering, it's straight into hospital.'

He kissed her then, gentle kisses, before adding, 'Not that children are important—not as long as I have you.'

And Kate relaxed in his arms—right where she belonged.

CHAPTER THIRTEEN

THEY MARRIED QUIETLY, asking a celebrant to perform the ceremony on the balcony of Angus's unit, Alice beside Kate and Angus's uncle supporting him.

'Your mother will be furious,' Alice told Kate, as she slipped on the long, linen shift she'd chosen for her wedding, flowers scattered on a cream background, including cornflowers that she loved and often took to wee Joshua's grave.

'I'll make peace with Mum,' Kate promised her aunt. 'We're already talking and when Angus has been at Bayside long enough to take some time off, we'll fly north to see them. He's already won some brownie points by being Scottish!'

Alice laughed and kissed Kate's cheek.

'Just be happy, both of you. I know it's trite and clichéd but make the most of every day and never be afraid to show your love.'

Too overcome for words, Kate kissed this woman who'd taken her in and probably saved her sanity.

Then they walked together out onto the balcony, looking out over the deep blue of the ocean and the white foam on the breakers closer to the shore.

Angus's smile and the pride in his eyes told Kate all she needed to know. She stood beside him, took his hand and said the words that would bind them together for ever.

'So, how do you like being Mrs Dr Caruth?' he asked as he bent his head and kissed her lips, gently yet firmly, promising so much more than words could ever convey.

Promising her love…

* * * * *

LET'S TALK
Romance

For exclusive extracts, competitions
and special offers, find us online:

📘 facebook.com/millsandboon

📷 @millsandboonuk

🐦 @millsandboon

Or get in touch on 0844 844 1351*

For all the latest titles coming soon,
visit millsandboon.co.uk/nextmonth

*Calls cost 7p per minute plus your phone company's price per
minute access charge

Want even more
ROMANCE?

Join our bookclub today!

'Mills & Boon books, the perfect way to escape for an hour or so.'

Miss W. Dyer

'Excellent service, promptly delivered and very good subscription choices.'

Miss A. Pearson

'You get fantastic special offers and the chance to get books before they hit the shops'

Mrs V. Hall

Visit millsandbook.co.uk/Bookclub and save on brand new books.

MILLS & BOON